"How d...
naked a... ...arlot!"

Nikolas's words were like an explosion.

"You've called me that before! I really think you'd like to believe it of me, wouldn't you, Nikolas?" taunted Bethany.

Once more his eyes raked over her body in the clinging wet cotton, and unconsciously she drew herself up proudly, tossing her hair.

"I'm your guardian and I expect you to obey me!" Nikolas's hand gripped her arm so hard that his strong fingers dug into her flesh. "You push me beyond endurance and I won't warn you again, Bethany. You don't realize the sort of situation you might provoke with your teasing!"

*But I do realize,* Bethany thought wildly. *What crazy demon is making me act this way, driving this man to his limits?* Her heart pounded as she wondered what might lie beyond those limits....

Other titles by
# REBECCA STRATTON
# IN HARLEQUIN ROMANCES

1942—THE FIRE AND THE FURY
1955—MOON TIDE
1976—THE GODDESS OF MAVISU
1991—ISLE OF THE GOLDEN DRUM
2006—PROUD STRANGER
2018—CHATEAU D'ARMOR
2036—THE ROAD TO GAFSA
2050—GEMINI CHILD
2078—GIRL IN A WHITE HAT
2091—INHERIT THE SUN
2106—MORE THAN A DREAM
2131—THE SIGN OF THE RAM
2141—THE VELVET GLOVE
2154—DREAM OF WINTER
2173—SPINDRIFT
2180—IMAGE OF LOVE
2201—BARGAIN FOR PARADISE
2222—CORSICAN BANDIT
2261—LOST HERITAGE
2268—THE EAGLE OF THE VINCELLA
2274—LARK IN AN ALIEN SKY
2303—CLOSE TO THE HEART
2339—THE TEARS OF VENUS

Other titles by
# REBECCA STRATTON
# IN HARLEQUIN PRESENTS

106—YELLOW MOON
121—THE WARM WIND OF FARIK

Many of these titles are available at your local bookseller.

For a free catalogue listing all available Harlequin Romances,
send your name and address to:

HARLEQUIN READER SERVICE,
M.P.O. Box 707, Niagara Falls, N.Y. 14302
Canadian address: Stratford, Ontario, Canada N5A 6W2

# Apollo's Daughter

by

## REBECCA STRATTON

## Harlequin Books

TORONTO • LONDON • LOS ANGELES • AMSTERDAM
SYDNEY • HAMBURG • PARIS • STOCKHOLM • ATHENS • TOKYO

Original hardcover edition published in 1980
by Mills & Boon Limited

ISBN 0-373-02356-1

Harlequin edition published September 1980

Copyright © 1980 by Rebecca Stratton.
Philippine copyright 1980. Australian copyright 1980.

All rights reserved. Except for use in any review, the reproduction or utilization
of this work in whole or in part in any form by any electronic, mechanical or
other means, now known or hereafter invented, including xerography,
photocopying and recording, or in any information storage or retrieval system,
is forbidden without the permission of the publisher. All the characters in this
book have no existence outside the imagination of the author and have no
relation whatsoever to anyone bearing the same name or names. They are not
even distantly inspired by any individual known or unknown to the author, and
all the incidents are pure invention.

The Harlequin trademark, consisting of the word HARLEQUIN and the
portrayal of a Harlequin, is registered in the United States Patent Office and in
the Canada Trade Marks Office.

Printed in U.S.A.

She remembered his first visit to Apolidus very
clearly indeed. She had been fourteen years old at the
⸻ the arrival of a big white motor cruiser in
⸻ used quite a stir, for it had
⸻ Meandis came from

# CHAPTER ONE

BETHANY could not really remember being anything
but Bethany Meandis or living anywhere but Apolidus, although she had in fact travelled extensively
during the first five years of her life. She knew very
little about her real father, except that he had been an
artist, and a skilled one, judging by the portrait of her
mother that Papa had kept even after she left them.
Megan Scott, her mother, had been a sculptor and
Bethany had inherited some of both parents' talents,
although she was a better painter than she was a sculptor.

At five years of age and living in the latest of a series
of artists' communes, Bethany's life had begun to
change when her father simply walked out one day
and did not come back. She supposed she had missed
him in a way, but her young mind was confused by so
many people sharing the somewhat casual care of the
numerous children in the commune, and she had not
been certain just who were her natural parents. Especially since neither Megan nor her father had been
very strong on parental affection or responsibility.

It was not until her mother remarried, when Bethany was seven, and Pavlos Meandis became her stepfather, that she really began to learn what true love
and affection were all about. Ten years older than his
new wife, and a widower, Pavlos gave to Bethany the
same generous love he gave his own tiny son, and she
had taken on the role of big sister quite happily for the
next eleven years.

Before long Pavlos had legally adopted her so that
she had been Bethany Meandis for almost as long as
she could remember, and she and Takis, her step-
brother, had thrived and grown up together in the
warm free atmosphere of Bethany's first real home.

Pavlos too was a sculptor, but to him his family came first and he loved both children equally.

Megan's departure, only four years after the marriage, had caused an upheaval and Pavlos had wept unashamedly, but Bethany, eleven at the time, had barely missed her, and her going had been less traumatic than Pavlos's much more recent death. He had been a caring man and his death had completely shattered her small world for some time, so that she was only just beginning to return to her normal lively and extrovert self. She was young and eager for life, and no one could mourn for ever, though the hurt was still there; and at eighteen there was so much to live for.

It was into her mood of returning normality that Aunt Alexia had dropped her bombshell. Bethany and Takis both being considered too young to cope alone, Pavlos had made arrangements for them to be put in the charge of his cousin from Rhodes, and Bethany's main fear was of being uprooted from what she had come to regard as her haven. After losing Papa, having to leave Apolidus would be the last straw, and she meant to dig in her heels if it came to the point.

Apolidus was a tiny island set among hundreds of others in the deep blue Aegean, and it supported a small colony of artists as well as the more traditional farming and fishing communities. Many of its seemingly perfect beaches were made dangerous by rocks that lurked beneath the water just off shore to the north and east of the island, and only on the south and west was it really safe to swim. The harbour faced south, towards the mainland of Greece, and was protected by high cliffs of pinkish rock, safe and secure when summer storms blew the sea into a raging fury, and the boats ran for shelter.

Aware of being watched, Bethany looked round. 'How much longer, Aunt Alex?'

She shifted uneasily on the box-seat in the window, not so much impatient as anxious, and Alexia Meandis smiled at the touchingly young profile once more out-

lined, cameo-pure, against the background of summer garden. 'Soon, child, soon,' she soothed, for the tenth time in scarcely more minutes.

Bethany returned to her v... busy with the eve...

...igil, but her mind was ...nts of the past year. A couple of times Papa had momentarily clouded the horizon of her contentment by raising the question of finding her a husband, but he had not pressed very hard and she had relaxed again. She did not have marriage in mind yet, even though she was past her eighteenth birthday, an age when most of the island girls already had some idea of who their future husbands would be.

Maybe, as well as consigning her guardianship to his cousin, Papa had also given him the task of finding her a husband, and at the thought of that being possible she again turned from the window and sought deliberately to banish the thought. 'He hasn't to rely on the ferry,' she complained to no one in particular. 'There's no earthly reason why he should be late when he has his own boat.'

Endowed with infinite patience, Alexia merely smiled, and Bethany again returned to her vigil. She felt rather like a schoolgirl again, waiting there with Takis, and both of them dressed in the Sunday best clothes they felt so uncomfortable in. Aunt Alexia had insisted that they look their smartest to meet their guardian, and looking their best to Alexia's traditional mind meant a stiff black skirt and bodice for Bethany, and her hair bound into a thick silky knot at the nape of her neck.

Bethany hated it and in part it added to her aversion to the man they sat waiting for so impatiently. She kept it firmly in mind that she, unlike Takis, was not a child, but eighteen years old, and she was not prepared to simply submit to a stranger walking in and taking over her life. Whether or not he was Papa's cousin and Papa had consigned their welfare to him made no difference, she was no longer a child. The fact that it was Nikolas Meandis who had been given such authority made it that much worse.

time and ~~the~~ ~~...~~
the tiny harbour had cause~~...~~
always been rumoured that Pavlos Mea~~...~~
a very wealthy family who now had little to do with
him. Nikolas himself had caused almost as much stir
too, for he had stalked along the quay to the Meandis
house with such an air of authority it might have been
supposed he owned the whole island.

No reason had been given for his coming when none
of the family had ever set foot on the island, except
for Aunt Alexia, but it was clear now, to Bethany at
least, why he had been there. Papa had known he had
not as long to live as most men, and he had made pre-
paration for her and Takis's care when he was gone.
Bethany had somehow never believed that the visit
was merely a social one, after all those years.

At fourteen she had thought herself grown-up, but
her pride had been badly dinted by the visitor's attitude. Nikolas Meandis, as she remembered him, was an
arrogant and self-opinionated man who obviously disapproved of the way she had been brought up and particularly of her stepfather's lenience towards her. But
when she mentioned her feeling to Papa later, he had
laughed and told her not to worry, that his cousin
was a good man. A traditionalist, perhaps, despite his
comparative youth, but a good man and a very wealthy
one.

Since that one brief visit Papa had seen nothing
more of Nikolas Meandis, and while she sat waiting
for his latest arrival Bethany pondered bitterly on the
irony of fate that had suddenly put her future into the
hands of a man who had so obviously disliked and disapproved of her. She fidgeted uneasily and once more
turned to look across the room at the old lady. 'How
much longer, Aunt Alex? He's very late!'

'No doubt with very good reason, child,' Alexia told
her, and took note of Bethany's nervous gesture of rubbing her hands down the stiff black skirt of her Sunday

best. 'Try not to be impatient, Bethany, he'll be here soon.'

'It isn't that I *want* to see him again,' Bethany insisted quickly. 'I didn't like him the last time he was here, and I'm sure he didn't like me, he made that very plain!'

'Bethany dear, the last time Niko was here was for your papa's funeral only two months ago,' Alexia reminded her, and added, with the slightest hint of reproach, 'You didn't see him then, of course.'

'I didn't see anyone,' Bethany agreed, her eyes distant. It was all too easy to recall that awful day when they had buried Papa in the small graveyard on the hillside above the village. Despite the whispers she knew must have been prevalent among the gathering of relatives and friends, she had been much too upset to do anything, and had gone to her room and stayed there. Alexia had coped as she always did, so patient and understanding. 'I don't remember him last time, but the time before that,' she insisted. 'I disliked him intensely, and I don't expect to feel any differently this time.'

'Bethany, my dear child!' Alexia shook her grey head in a gesture more of regret than censure, and her voice was gentle and quiet as it always was. 'You should not form opinions on old memories. Wait until you meet Niko again before you declare yourself so firmly; it isn't reasonable and it can only make things more difficult for you.'

Bethany appreciated that she might be right, but she doubted if Aunt Alexia realised quite how she felt about the man they were waiting for. Alexia was elderly and a little unworldly at times. The widow of Pavlos's uncle, she had come willingly to care for her nephew-in-law and his children when Bethany's mother left them, and she had stayed on even after Bethany was old enough to take over from her. She had never had children of her own and she doted on both the young people, never allowing them to do any-

thing for themselves, and spoiling them quite shamelessly.

Sitting back in the coolest part of the low-ceilinged
room, she busied herself with sewing, for she was an
accomplished embroideress, and she shook her head
over Bethany's present attitude. It was not good for a
young woman to show such defiance as showed in
Bethany's eyes and in the angle of her chin, and it was
to be regretted more than ever in the present situation.

'It's simply that I know what to expect,' Bethany insisted. 'He made no attempt to hide his opinion of me
when he came here the first time, and now that he's to
be our guardian——' She shrugged uneasily. 'He
wouldn't have minded so much if I'd been Greek, but
he didn't approve of Papa adopting a foreigner.'

'Oh, Bethany, my dear child!' Alexia rested her
work on her lap for the moment and looked across at
her concernedly. 'You're as Greek as anyone could be
who wasn't actually born here, and I'm sure Niko was
never so uncharitable as to think anything else.'

'Maybe not.' Bethany made the allowance because
she was Greek enough to realise how serious her charge
was to a people steeped in the traditions of hospitality,
but she did not really believe it.

'You even speak Greek,' Alexia reminded her, and for
a second Bethany's lips trembled slightly, for she again
felt that awful sense of loss.

'Always since Papa died,' she murmured, and twisted
her fingers together on her lap, hating the drabness of
the stiff black skirt suddenly. 'He always talked to me in
English for a little every day, because he said I should
never forget my background.' Her hands were unsteady and to try and steady them she clasped them
more tightly together, swallowing hard because she did
not want to cry any more. 'I wish I *was* Greek, Aunt
Alex, and then I wouldn't feel so much like a stranger.'

The sunlight coming in through the open window
gave her hair the colour and sheen of burnished
bronze, neither blonde nor red, and she had never
looked less like the other girls on the island, a fact that

for once she regretted. Her mother had been fair and pretty, but Bethany's features had the classical perfection more often associated with the ancient beauties of her adopted country.

Her skin was lighter than the golden-brown Greek complexion, although it had darkened to a pale creamy bronze after years in the Grecian sun, and the contours of her face were clear and neatly defined. Her mouth full and soft and her nose small and straight, while her brows were drawn on two finely arched crescents above huge grey eyes. Her stepfather had often remarked that she had the looks of the ancient goddesses, and promised that one day she would cause as much havoc among men. At the moment she looked very young and much too defiantly anxious, and Alexia Meandis smiled at her comfortingly.

'Do you feel such a stranger, child?' she asked gently, and Bethany shook her head without looking at her.

'Only when I remember how that man—how Cousin Nikolas looked at me,' she said.

'You have such an imagination, child,' Alexia chided gently. 'I'm quite sure that Niko was enchanted with you, as we all are. He is a stern man, I know, but not as hard and unreasonable as you seem to think.'

'Maybe.' Bethany was unconvinced, and she caught Takis's eye when he turned from the window for a moment. 'Do you remember him, Takis? From that first time he came?'

Takis was twelve years old and tall and thin for his age, but his smile had the same warmth and charm his father's had had. Secretly, Bethany suspected, he was as much excited as resentful at the prospect of Nikolas Meandis's arrival, for all he claimed to dislike the idea of having a guardian. His black hair curled slightly and grew low over his brow, and he had a habit of running his fingers through it sometimes, as he did before he answered her.

'I think I quite liked him,' he said, and Bethany stared at him in disbelief.

'You were frightened of him,' she declared, and saw

nothing tactless in reminding him of his childish awe. 'You said you thought he was cruel.'

With all the conscious superiority of the Greek male, Takis frowned disapprovingly. 'I was only a child,' he reminded her. 'And I wasn't frightened of him, Beth, I quite liked him.'

The retort Bethany had ready died on her lips when she caught Alexia's eye. 'Much better to forget past impressions,' the old lady advised, 'and be as polite and charming as I know you both can be. I know you find it hard to be as retiring as a man like Niko expects of his womenfolk, my child, but remember that it cannot be easy for Niko either. It cannot be an easy thing to suddenly become the guardian of two young people whom he must know feel a certain amount of resentment; and remember that this situation is, after all, none of his choosing.'

'I suppose not.'

Bethany admitted it reluctantly, but she could see that for Alexia's sake she ought to make the effort and accept the situation with as good grace as possible. Takis was obviously prepared to accept it, at least for the moment, and she did not want to appear ill-mannered and deliberately unco-operative.

Impulsive as always, she went across and hugged the old lady affectionately, for her generous and outgoing nature found it easier on the whole to give anyone the benefit of the doubt whenever possible. 'I'll be an absolute paragon, Aunt Alex,' she told her extravagantly. 'I promise.'

'Dear little one,' Alexia smiled affectionately, 'just be yourself, and for papa's sake try to love his cousin.'

'He's coming!' Takis leapt up from the long wooden seat in the window, scattering cushions in his haste. 'Beth, he looks even bigger than I remember, and—— Do you suppose he really *is* as stern as he looks?'

Already Bethany could feel the increased urgency of her heartbeat, banging away at her ribs, and she bit anxiously on her bottom lip as she automatically brushed down her skirt. Visitors were always heralded by the sound of footsteps, for the path that curved around the little garden from the arched gateway in the wall was made up of coloured pebbles, and even the softest heels clicked busily on the uneven surfaces. The tread she heard now was firm and somehow slightly ominous, and she exchanged swift, anxious glances with Takis. She would have given anything for Papa's comforting presence.

Alexia was already at the door, standing tall and handsome in her black patterned dress, with her grey hair coiled neatly in the nape of her neck. She smiled a welcome, but so far Bethany could not see the man she welcomed for the open door that hid him from her view. All she saw of him were two large brown hands that clasped the old lady's with gentle firmness, then transferred their hold to her arms and drew her into an embrace.

'Welcome,' Alexia murmured, smiling warmly. 'Welcome, nephew. Health to you!'

For a second Bethany glimpsed a dark head bent to kiss the old lady on both cheeks, but then he vanished once again behind the concealing door, and she had still not seen him properly. She waited impatiently until Alexia stood aside to let him in, and he followed her into the big sprawling cottage room, seeming to diminish its size the moment he walked into it.

Her first glimpse of him surprised her, for she had somehow expected an older man. Then she recalled that she had been only fourteen years old at their last meeting, and he must then have been approaching thirty, her own maturity made a difference to her view of him. He was handsome in a sternly rugged way, like her stepfather, but lacking Pavlos's quick warmth and charm. His eyes were dark and his mouth firm and straight, though slightly full in the lower lip, suggesting a sensuality that was somehow startling and unexpected. A fringe of thick black lashes slightly softened the effect of an otherwise implacable face.

He was about thirty-two or three, Bethany guessed, but there was nothing about him that she found re-

assuring, for he looked every bit as formidable as she
remembered him, and now she did not have Papa to
take the edge off his disapproval. Standing with her
hands grasping the stiff black stuff of her Sunday skirt,
she glanced at him from below tawny lashes while he
moved across to where she and Takis stood side by
side.

'Takis!' The boy's hand was firmly clasped and
shaken, then he was drawn into a bear-hug while a
hand patted his back. It was a greeting and sympathy
in one firm gesture, and oddly touching to witness
somehow. 'How are you, cousin?'

'Well, thank you.' Takis sounded very grown-up and
formal and Bethany, who knew him well, guessed he
was still feeling his way; trying to make up his mind.
'Are you well, cousin?'

Aunt Alexia moved up beside the tall, towering
figure as he turned towards Bethany, and her gentle
voice slipped in before the newcomer could say anything. 'You remember Bethany, don't you, Niko?' she
reminded him, and her light fingers touched Bethany's
in gentle reminder as she smiled at her. 'She is a grown
woman now, as you see.'

Nikolas Meandis extended a hand that engulfed
her own slim fingers, his steady gaze fixed on her and,
to Bethany's sensitive mind, already critical. 'I believe
I saw you briefly at Pavlos's funeral,' he said. 'How
are you, Bethany?'

His greeting seemed friendly enough and she relaxed just a little, a slight smile touching the soft contours of her mouth for a moment as she answered. 'I'm
well, thank you, cousin; are you?'

She would have sworn that he frowned over her use
of the familiar cousin, although she did not look at
him to confirm it. She was very thankful that he didn't
kiss her as he had Alexia, but merely contented himself with a handshake, and she heaved an inward sigh
of relief that the first encounter had been less discomfiting than she had anticipated.

Ever the watchful hostess, Alexia offered the tradi-

tional hospitality. 'You will take *Ioukoumi*?' she
offered. 'And coffee?'

'Thank you, I will.'

While Alexia left them to go to the kitchen, Bethany
sat down with Takis and the newcomer, just as she always did when there was company; Alexia had never
wanted it any other way. But when Bethany sat down
as well, instead of following her aunt into the kitchen,
Nikolas Meandis eyed her curiously for a moment.

For the first time ever, Bethany felt like an outsider.
Something in those watching eyes reminded her that
Takis was a blood relation while she was merely
adopted into the Meandis family. But it was possible
that he wanted to talk to Takis alone, man to man, so
she got up from her chair, murmuring an excuse, and
went to find Alexia in the kitchen. 'I think they want
to talk about Papa,' she explained when Alexia looked
up, obviously surprised at her appearance.

'Very possibly,' Alexia agreed, then went on with
her preparations, glancing only briefly to judge Bethany's expression when she sought her opinion. 'You see
now how wrong you were about Niko, child?'

Unwilling to be committed so soon, Bethany shrugged. She put soft, sticky Turkish delight into a dish,
then licked the powdery white sugar from her fingers
before setting the dish on the tray her aunt was preparing. 'Maybe,' she allowed cautiously. 'But I'd rather
wait and see what happens before I make up my mind,
Aunt Alex.'

As it happened, her caution was justified sooner
than she expected. For it was after they had enjoyed
the excellent lunch that Alexia had made them and yet
more coffee was required that Nikolas Meandis made it
quite clear what was in store for her. He could have
no further need to talk alone with Takis, and he had
expounded his opinions during lunch in such a way
that none of them was left in any doubt that he was
every bit as traditionally minded as Papa had suggested. When Alexia got up to fetch the coffee, he

again looked across at Bethany with the same suggestion of disapproval.

'Surely your help is needed to prepare the coffee?'
he suggested, and for the moment Bethany did not see
the trap she was stepping into.

Smiling, she shook her head. 'Oh no, it's all right,'
she told him in her blithe innocence. 'Aunt Alex al-
way does it.'

It took her a moment or two to realise what kind of
view he would take of the situation and she felt herself
colouring furiously when she realised. He had no idea
that Alexia did such jobs herself because she preferred
it that way, and she could see that he merely saw it as
another indication of her too lenient upbringing.

'Then I suggest it is time Aunt Alexia had some
assistance,' he told her in a quiet, firm voice.

The place for women was in the kitchen, not sitting
with the men and waiting to be served; his opinion
was clear enough, and Bethany's cheeks were burning
as she got hastily to her feet. She almost ran from the
room with her hands clenched tightly against the stiff
blackness of her skirt, and a churning hardness like a
lead weight in her stomach.

In the kitchen, bright with copper pans and scarlet
geraniums in pots, Alexia turned curiously to see who
had followed her, and when she saw Bethany's flushed
cheeks and suspiciously bright eyes, she came across to
her, her gentle face anxious and enquiring. 'Bethany
child, what's wrong?'

Struggling for a moment with mingled anger and
humiliation, Bethany stood by the kitchen table, her
clenched hands pressed on to the scrubbed wooden
top. 'I have to help you with the coffee,' she managed
in a small strangled voice. 'Aunt Alex, you know I'd
help you if you wanted me to, but you never will——'
She swallowed hard, fighting the need to cry with every
nerve in her body, and shaking like a leaf. 'Oh, he's
every bit as bad as I remember him! He thinks I'm
lazy and spoiled, and he still despises me as he did
that other time. He'll be awful to me, I know he will!

Oh, Aunt Alex, I *hate* him! I hate him and I won't stay and be treated like—like a—I'll go away! He can't stop me; I'm old enough, he can't stop me!'

'Bethany, little one!'

Alexia's dark eyes were troubled and she took the small clenched hands in hers, trying to ease their angry tension with her gentle fingers. If Bethany had not been suffering so much from hurt pride and a sense of injustice, she would have noticed the old lady's concern and realised that with her outburst she was simply making a difficult situation worse. But her sympathy was turned inward at the moment, and her spirit revolted against being so pointedly blamed for her shortcomings, rather than against being expected to help.

'You mustn't talk like that,' Alexia insisted gently. 'You cannot go away, child, when it was your papa's wish that you stay.'

'It wasn't Papa's wish that I should be reprimanded for something not my fault, and made to look small before that man had been in the house five minutes!' Bethany insisted in a voice that rose despite her efforts to control it. 'He doesn't like me, Aunt Alex, any more than he did the first time he came here, and I can't— I *won't* stay and be treated like a——'

'Like a spoiled child?' a deep quiet voice enquired from the doorway, and Bethany swung quickly round, her eyes bright and shimmering with tears. 'I could not help but overhear,' Nikolas Meandis informed her. He stood just inside the kitchen with one hand in a pocket, and looking deceptively cool and casual until one looked at the gleaming darkness of his eyes. 'I wasn't aware that I was being unreasonable by suggesting you help with making the coffee,' he went on. 'It's surely one of the tasks a woman normally does about the house, isn't it?'

'It isn't really necessary for Bethany to help, Niko,' Alexia told him in her gently persuasive voice, but he would hear no opinion but his own firmly established one.

'Bethany is no longer a child, Aunt Alexia,' he told the old lady quietly. 'She is a woman and perfectly capable of doing a woman's work; it isn't reasonable that you should still be working as you do while Bethany——'

'I would help!' Bethany interrupted, huskily angry, and the interruption brought the dark gaze back to her.

'Then you will make the coffee while I discuss some matters with Aunt Alexia,' Nikolas decreed. 'Do you know how to make coffee?'

Fuming, but keeping Alexia's cautionary warning in mind, Bethany nodded. Never since her early childhood had she been spoken to so harshly, and she resented it because she considered it uncalled-for. 'Yes, of course I know how to make coffee!'

'Then please do so while I talk to Aunt Alexia,' Nikolas said, and moved across to his aunt, taking her arm and firmly edging her towards the door. 'Later on I shall wish to speak to you as well, Bethany, but that can wait. It seems there's a great deal that needs to be discussed if I'm to make a success of being guardian to you and Takis.'

'Not necessarily to me,' Bethany denied swiftly. 'I'm not really your responsibility, I'm not even Greek in fact——'

'You're Greek by adoption,' Nikolas insisted, and his eyes narrowed as if he sought the reason for her sudden denial of her adopted country. 'By adopting you, my cousin made you a member of our family, therefore you are my responsibility, whether you like it or not, and I shall see that you do nothing to bring shame on my family's name.'

'By being independent?' Bethany guessed, and Nikolas looked at her steadily.

'By being unfeminine and wilful,' he corrected her quietly. 'When the coffee is ready we'll have it outside, if you please.'

Bethany turned on him and her eyes blazed with the fury of frustration, her cheeks bright with colour. If only Alexia had not been there she would have told him exactly what she thought of him. Not that she had anything at all against helping Aunt Alexia or of making the coffee and serving it, but she hated his high-handed way of stressing her lack of, as he saw it, feminine qualities.

'You——'

'Outside, if you please,' Nikolas stressed firmly, and looked down at her with a harsh determined gleam in his eyes that was completely at variance with the gentle way he treated his aunt.

Her hands were trembling and Bethany had never felt so shiveringly angry in her life before, but she caught the look of appeal in Alexia's eyes for a moment and swallowed hard on the response she had ready. Without another word she turned and walked across the kitchen with her head high, thankful that at least he could not see the suspicion of tears in her eyes or he might have misconstrued their cause. For the moment she could see no other way but to do as he said, but she would think of something, she swore she would.

Bethany had helped to wash up and to prepare dinner, and provided coffee whenever it was required. Rather surprisingly her coffee seemed to be the best she had ever made and she wondered if she had unconsciously made more of an effort than she usually did, just to prove to Nikolas Meandis that she was not as lazy and incompetent as he obviously thought her.

What she did not relish, the following morning, was taking out his breakfast to him in the garden, but Alexia had thought it would be a gesture that showed her willingness to work as hard as anyone. Alexia herself deliberately delayed her own arrival and it was never easy to get Takis out of bed in the morning, so that the only ones astir that bright hot morning were Bethany and the hated newcomer.

Discarding the drab formality of black, she blossomed out in one of the light, thin, gaily coloured

dresses she more normally wore, and her hair was freed
of the severe knot to blow around her face in the soft
morning breeze as she walked out on to the little stone
terrace. The tray she carried held fresh-baked rolls as
well as coffee, and a pot of their own honey, sweet and
golden, prepared by Aunt Alexia.

Her slim legs were bare and her sandalled feet slapped lightly on the paved ground while she concentrated on keeping the tray balanced evenly. She almost
dropped it when two much larger hands reached out
for it and took it from her. 'Good morning, Bethany.'

She muttered a reply, following Nikolas to the small
wooden table set below the garden's one tall plane
tree, and he did not, she noted, make a move to help
further once he had put down the tray on the table.
Sitting down, he sat back in his chair and crossed his
long legs one over the other, regarding her for a moment in silence.

'You no longer wear mourning,' he said, and instinctively Bethany's hand tightened on the handle of
the little *briki* of coffee so that it banged down on to
the table much more firmly than she intended.

'Papa never liked mourning,' she told him, and
noticed how anxious her voice sounded. She did not
want to begin disagreeing with him this early in the
day, and for Alexia's sake she vowed she would not.
'It isn't any disrespect, Nikolas, we—we just don't
think that way.'

'I understand.' His words startled her, and she stared
at him, but he seemed unaware of the effect he had,
and eyed the little basket of bread rolls with apparent
interest. 'Did you make these?'

Bethany nodded, wondering what his verdict would
be, for bread-making was not her strong point. Setting
a plate and a cup and saucer in front of him with the
usual accompanying glass of water, she supposed she
had better enlarge on her admission. He would discover soon enough just how successful she had been.

'I'm not very good at bread,' she admitted, with a

hint of defiance. 'But you said I was to give Aunt Alex a hand and I have.'

For a moment he said nothing, helping himself to coffee while she stood there watching him. Then he looked up at her and she thought there was a suspicion of a smile about his mouth before he spoke. 'Do you so dislike domesticity, Bethany?'

'No.' She felt awkward, schoolgirlish, and she resented the feeling mostly because he was causing it. 'I just don't like being blamed for something that isn't my fault, that's all.'

'Ah!' He sipped his coffee, thick and black and unsweetened, she noticed. Then he looked at the tray before glancing up at her again. 'Am I to breakfast alone? Aren't you or the others coming to join me?'

Bethany was so tempted to tell him that she knew her place better than to suppose she was allowed to eat in his company, but she held her tongue for the sake of peace. 'Aunt Alex isn't quite ready,' she told him, 'and Takis isn't up yet.'

'And you?' He asked the question softly, holding the coffee cup between his big hands while he looked at her. 'Don't you eat breakfast, Bethany, or are you simply making an exception of this occasion?'

'I do; of course I do.'

She held the empty tray in front of her looking oddly defensive and finding it easier not to meet his eyes. 'Then fetch yourself a cup and saucer and a plate and have breakfast with me,' Nikolas told her. 'I'm not used to eating alone and I find it rather lonely.'

Bethany did as he said and brought herself the necessary implements before she questioned his meaning about being lonely. 'Do you have a large family?' she asked, and hastily avoided the dark-eyed glance that questioned her.

'If you mean have I a lot of children,' he told her, biting into one of her crusty rolls, 'I am not married, Bethany.' Somehow it was so difficult to avoid looking at him, and again she caught his eyes before hastily avoiding them. 'Did you think I was?' he asked.

Bethany stirred sugar into her coffee with an entirely automatic gesture, trying to decide just how much she did know about him. It was little enough, she had to admit, for Papa had not been one to talk about his absent family. But Nikolas Meandis was over thirty and she had to allow that he was an attractive man, even though it was a rather austere kind of attraction, and apart from that it was customary for a man of his age to be married and have a family.

'I naturally assumed you were,' she told him after a few seconds' consideration.

'Did you?' She found those dark eyes across the table very disconcerting, and wished herself anywhere but sharing a table with him. 'What are your own feelings about marriage, Bethany?'

To say that she was surprised was understating her reaction, and Bethany stared at him wide-eyed for a moment, then shook her head. She was again reminded of her stepfather's tentative mention of the subject not long before he died, but if finding a husband for her was one of the tasks he had entrusted to his cousin then she might as well tell him her own feelings about it right away.

'I have no intention of marrying anyone I don't love,' she informed him in as firm a voice as she could manage in the circumstances. 'I don't intend being married off to just anyone, like most of the island girls are, Nikolas, I might as well tell you that right from the beginning. When I meet a man I want to marry, then I'll marry him, but until I do—no!'

'I see.'

His quiet acceptance of it was unexpected too, and again she eyed him warily as he helped himself to another bread roll. Dipping in to the honey, he transferred some to his plate, then twirled the sticky golden mess round and round the blade of his knife, and he seemed to be thinking deeply about something, so that his next words took her rather by surprise.

'Your bread rolls are excellent, Bethany. You must have a natural aptitude, since you don't normally help with the baking; and you have no reason at all to suggest you're not very good.'

It was annoying to realise she was blushing at the compliment and Bethany wished she did not feel quite so pleased about it. 'Aunt Alex is a good teacher,' she told him. 'But it's more luck than skill that they've turned out well.'

He watched her while he ate, and she found the steady scrutiny of those heavy-lashed eyes very discomfiting, wishing she had found some excuse for not joining him, however pressing the invitation. 'Do compliments embarrass you?' he asked, so quietly and matter-of-factly, and Bethany squirmed uncomfortably on her chair. If only Takis or Aunt Alex would come out and join them, for she found this dark, quietly confident man a very disturbing breakfast companion.

Trying to appear offhand, she lightly raised one shoulder and shook her head. 'I'm not used to strangers paying me compliments,' she confessed with disarming frankness, and he appeared not to resent being classed as a stranger, only smiled faintly to himself.

'Perhaps because you've met so few,' he suggested. He continued with his meal and seemed not to notice that Bethany was getting rather less enjoyment from hers. 'There are certain matters I shall want to discuss as soon as I've been through Pavlos's things more thoroughly,' he went on. 'Takis is rather too young to be included, but you're eighteen and old enough to make an intelligent contribution to the conversation, I'm sure.'

Yet again he had caught her unprepared, and she hesitated, taking a fortifying sip from her coffee before she replied. 'I'm sure I could,' she agreed eventually, 'but I hardly expected to be given the opportunity in this instance. What reason do you have, Nikolas?'

'Meaning?'

The demand was abrupt and as sharp as the gleam in his eyes when he looked across at her. 'Well, I would have thought I was the last person you'd think of sitting down to a discussion with, when you——'

She bit back the words hastily, but it was too late, he must have followed her meaning easily and his mouth had that tight and slightly ominous look she had noticed just after he arrived. 'I had the impression that you find me rather too conservative for your taste,' he told her, 'but apparently you're not prepared to accept an effort on my part to remedy the impression. Instead you question my motives!'

It was a tricky situation and one Bethany was new to, she wasn't sure just how to handle it at the moment. Licking traces of honey from her lips, she shook her head slowly in automatic denial, seeing any advantage she might have had slipping away from her. 'I wasn't exactly questioning your motives,' she claimed huskily. 'I only meant that it isn't like you to ask the opinion of any woman——'

'You know me so well?'

She shook her head more certainly this time. 'No, but I know your type.'

He was almost certainly angry, it showed in his eyes and the tight firmness of his mouth, but he had himself firmly under control and his voice was almost coolly matter-of-fact. 'I am forced to the conclusion that you're not only spoiled but deliberately provocative on occasion,' he decreed, 'but don't try provoking me too far, Bethany, or you'll find yourself very, very sorry indeed!'

Bethany did her best to keep a firm hold on her own fiery temper, but she was flushed and growing angry, resenting his accusations the more because they came uncomfortably near the truth in part. 'I was just remembering that Papa referred to you as a traditionalist,' she told him. 'I know you have different ideas about how people should behave——'

'I believe that people, and particularly young people, should behave properly and with due respect for others,' Nikolas informed her curtly. 'My cousin was a very kindly man, and he was loved for his kindness, but he was in my opinion much too lax in the upbringing of his children.'

'You mean he should have beaten us as you would have done?' Bethany guessed bitterly, and saw the watching dark eyes narrow into glittering anger.

'I would remind you that it is still not too late to begin!' Nikolas threatened her.

Flushed and shaking like a leaf, Bethany sought to steady herself by taking a long drink from her coffee cup and somehow managed to hold her tongue until she was more under control. He was impossible, even more impossible than she had feared, and she could not foresee there being any improvement in their situation as long as he persisted in treating her the way he would a fractious child. She had never, since she could remember, had any trouble making the few men she came into contact with see things her way, and Nikolas, being the exception, not only angered her but, she had to admit, intrigued her.

Holding her cup between both hands, she studied his implacable face surreptitiously while he poured himself more coffee. Noting how the clear morning sun showed up fine lines at the corners of his eyes, and cast intriguing shadows below high cheekbones and thick black lashes, that were far too feminine for such a ruggedly masculine face. There was an almost oriental look about him that fitted his chauvinistic attitude, and she knew he would never be as amenable as Papa had been.

'It isn't going to work, Nikolas,' she declared impulsively, and met his eyes when he looked across at her suddenly. 'You and I under the same roof, it isn't going to work.'

His gaze did not waver, but it was several seconds before he replied and Bethany barely suppressed a shiver at something she glimpsed in the depth of his eyes for a moment. 'It will work,' he told her with firm assurance. 'I will *make* it work—and so will you.'

Bethany shook her head, though it was less in denial than at his incredible confidence, for despite her expressed doubts, she had the strangest feeling that he might be right.

# CHAPTER TWO

It was some time since Bethany had visited Pavlos's studio. She had done so quite often when her stepfather was alive, but she had never yet summoned the nerve to go in there since he died. It was as if she feared a recurrence of that dreadful sense of loss when she found he was no longer there to welcome her, and so far had avoided it.

She wasn't certain just what prompted her to go on that particular morning, unless it was because she had passed outside the window earlier and a glimpse of the familiar room had drawn her to it unthinkingly. She hesitated before turning the handle and opening the door, and when she found it not deserted, as she expected, she gasped aloud, staring across at Nikolas sitting at the rough wooden table that had done Pavlos service for a desk on the rare occasions he needed one.

Nikolas looked up when the door opened and his eyes narrowed slightly, so that she half expected a reprimand for intruding. He had a pile of papers in front of him and even from the doorway Bethany could recognise her stepfather's big, ungainly handwriting. It caught at her susceptible emotions for a moment, and she felt a flicker of resentment at the idea of Nikolas invading the privacy of the papers she knew Pavlos had kept in a steel box in one of the table drawers.

'I didn't know you were here,' she murmured, and prepared to withdraw, but Nikolas shook his head, calling out to her as the door began to close.

'Don't go, Bethany, come in and close the door.' Seeing her hesitate, he frowned and threw rather than put down the bundle of papers he had in his hand, before he sat down. 'Aunt Alexia will be here in a moment, you have no need to look so apprehensive! Sit down, I'm sure we won't be very long waiting.'

'Why here?' Bethany asked, vaguely uneasy at the turn events had taken suddenly. 'Why not in the living room where it's more comfortable?'

'You find your stepfather's studio discomfiting?'

She met his eyes, briefly surprised by the suggestion, then shook her head jerkily from side to side. 'Of course I don't, but——'

'Then please sit down; Aunt Alexia will join us when she is ready.' He met her eyes again and his gaze was boldly challenging, daring her to find further fault with the arrangement. 'In fact it was Aunt Alexia's suggestion that we talk in here, since I was already here with all Pavlos's things on hand, and she had no objection to returning here.'

Obediently Bethany drew up a chair and seated herself on the other side of the little table from him, heaving an inward sigh of relief when Alexia put in her appearance almost immediately. She smiled at them both with her usual benign assurance, and Nikolas at once got to his feet and set the most comfortable chair in the room for her, next to his own, while she watched him obliquely.

It was odd to feel the room so familiar and yet so unfamiliar with Nikolas's intruding presence, and she found it hard to keep her mind on present matters when the room reminded her so much of Papa. It was a big sunny room untidily tacked on to the original building and having a long window that opened on to the small terrace where they ate most of their meals.

Beyond it was the garden at the back of the house. A rambling untidy garden that ran riot with pink oleanders and scarlet hibiscus; where jasmine struggled to find the warming sun through rampant greenery, and great curtains of purple bougainvillaea trailed over the walls that enclosed house and garden. A thriving fig tree strayed over the wall, a struggling palm, almost defeated by so much opposition, and the big plane tree shading the terrace. A private jungle, her stepfather had called it, and remembering his laughter, Bethany smiled to herself.

The room itself was workmanlike, filled with the usual stuff of the sculptor. The tools, left where they were last used, were a poignant reminder of their late owner, and several finished heads in marble as well as terracotta bore silent witness to the skill of Pavlos Meandis. The partially finished bust of a village child stood wrapped in wet cloths, waiting in vain to be finished, and that, perhaps more than anything else, brought home the cold, hard fact of his loss.

On the wall facing Nikolas hung the portrait of her mother, painted by her true father, and as she mostly did when she came to the studio, Bethany half turned her head to look at it. The face was pretty but it lacked beauty, and there was a boldness in the grey eyes that, combined with a curious half-smile, had the same discomfiting effect as the Mona Lisa if you looked at it for very long.

Nikolas noticed her interest in it and briefly he too gave it his attention. 'That's your mother, isn't it, Bethany?' he said, and she nodded.

She wasn't quite sure why his knowledge surprised her, for Papa was quite likely to have told him when he came that first time. 'My father painted it,' she told him, turning to look at the painting more fully. 'It's very good, isn't it? Don't you think she was pretty, Nikolas?'

'She was pretty,' Nikolas agreed in a cool, offhand voice, 'but she wasn't beautiful, as her daughter is. Are you perhaps like your father, Bethany?'

The unexpected compliment startled her into gazing at him uncertainly for a moment, for she saw such response as out of character for him, and she was unsure how to react. Aunt Alexia's blandly gentle face offered no solution, and she eventually shrugged in assumed carelessness, sidestepping his opinion of her own looks and simply answering his question as well as she could. Her father was a subject she knew virtually nothing about, though she was reluctant to admit it.

'Probably I am,' she said.

'Don't you remember him?'

'I was only five when he left us,' she told him. 'Mother married Papa when I was seven and I've virtually forgotten everything before that.' She looked across at him with a gleam of defiance in her grey eyes. 'I don't even know his first name, he was never mentioned.'

Nikolas was spreading the papers out on the table in front of him while he spoke and seemed to be consulting them. 'Your mother died about three years ago, didn't she?' He glanced up suddenly, as if something had just occurred to him. 'I'm sorry, I shouldn't have been quite so—abrupt about it.'

'It doesn't matter.' She tightened her hands in her lap and shook her head quickly. 'I never really knew her very well. She was killed in an accident, about three years ago, as you said.'

'But you hadn't seen her for several years before that?'

'No, I hadn't. She went off and left us, just as my father did.' She said it without bitterness, because neither of her natural parents had meant as much to her as Pavlos did, and she would have felt far more betrayed if it had been he who went off and left her. Nevertheless she felt oddly vulnerable for a moment and had a need to strike out in defence. 'You sound like a lawyer,' she accused, and ignored Alexia's faintly indrawn breath that should have warned her. 'Questions, questions! Just like a lawyer!'

Nikolas was more than equal to the task of dealing with her, however, and his controlled quietness had the inevitable effect of bringing her swiftly back to earth. Leaning his elbows on the table in front of him, he steepled his long fingers and looked at her steadily either side of them. 'If you wished to be offensive, I'm afraid you've failed,' he told her. 'I was trained in law school before I entered our family business, Bethany, so you're quite right. I *do* sound like a lawyer, for the very simple reason that I am one.'

There was too much she didn't know about him, Bethany thought, and could not think why it seemed to

matter so much. She ventured an upward glance only
when she thought his interest might be engaged else-
where, but she had misjudged. He was watching her
still with a deep, dark look in his eyes that she could
make nothing of, but which brought a curious little
shiver to her skin.

'I didn't know,' she said, and quite unwittingly
made it an apology.

'Obviously,' Nikolas remarked coolly. 'And now that
you do will you allow me to continue, or shall I discuss
these matters with Aunt Alexia only, and assume that
you are, after all, too immature to be included?'

Bethany flushed and her hands clenched into fists on
her lap, but she knew Alexia was silently pleading
with her not to quarrel with him, so she took a firm
hold on herself, nodding without looking up. 'I'm
sorry; please go on, Nikolas.'

A brief nod acknowledged her apology, and he
rested his elbows on the table while he talked. 'I ask
all these questions simply because I know so little
about you,' he explained. 'And since I am—in the
position I'm in, I feel I should know all about you.
You were about fifteen when your mother died, yes?'

'Yes, she went off when I was about eleven and left
me here with Papa, and it was about four years after
that that Papa heard she'd been killed in a car crash
in Rome. We—Papa had her brought back here and
she was buried in the artists' cemetery; he was—I think
he was still very fond of her.'

She could not claim to have mourned her mother,
and she thought he understood that, just as he understood that Papa had mourned her even after all those
years, and that was why he still kept her portrait in
his studio. 'I have been mother to both Pavlos's little
ones for more than seven years now, Niko,' Alexia reminded him in her quiet, gentle voice, and Bethany
noted how his expression changed whenever he looked
at or spoke to his aunt.

'I know, my aunt,' he told her, and there was a hint
of dryness in his voice that matched the faintly sar-

donic smile he gave her, 'and you have been more indulgent than most mothers. Have you always done
everything yourself, without Bethany's assistance?'

'Only because I wished to,' Alexia assured him
quickly. 'It isn't necessary for Bethany to do anything
and I am accustomed to working alone, Niko. Bethany's time will come soon enough.'

'Which is all the more reason why she should begin
training for the part of wife and mother,' Nikolas insisted gently, and turned his head when he caught
Bethany's hastily indrawn breath. 'How do you occupy
your time, Bethany? Do you sew?'

'A little.' She glanced anxiously at Alexia, for she
disliked this particular trend of conversation intensely.
'Mostly I paint, or sculpt a little, when we're not
swimming, or digging.'

'Digging?'

Bethany wondered if she should have mentioned
that, for so far only she and Takis knew of their very
amateurish efforts at archaeology, but she was glad
enough to steer him away from the subject of her
domestic shortcomings. 'There's a small hollow in the
side of the hill above the harbour,' she explained, 'and
Takis and I think there might once have been a temple
there; to Apollo, we think. We've only done a little,
but we've——'

'You have a permit?'

Oh, that lawyer's mind! Bethany looked at him and
then at Aunt Alexia. 'I didn't think it was necessary
for the little we do.'

'You still need permission,' he told her, then abruptly changed the subject. 'Takis is still at school, of
course. Have you finished your schooling?'

It was a matter she preferred not to talk about, for
she felt sometimes that she had disappointed Pavlos
with her academic record. Like all Greeks he had set
great store by a good education, and she had not taken
advantage of what opportunity she had. Rubbing her
hands down her skirt, she did not meet his eyes.

'I wasn't a very good pupil and sometimes I didn't

go. Papa sometimes taught me a little instead, but he never scolded me, or not very much.'

The dark eyes watching her gleamed with disapproval. 'You should have been made to go to school and punished when you did not,' Nikolas declared firmly. 'Discipline appears to have been non-existent, and my cousin appears to have indulged you to the point of foolishness. All of which is going to make my task even more difficult than I feared.'

His air of authority as much as his criticism of Papa annoyed Bethany, and she looked at him down her nose, leaving her feelings in no doubt. 'I've already said you needn't concern yourself with me,' she told him pertly. 'I'm eighteen years old and I don't need a guardian!'

'On the contrary,' Nikolas argued. 'Not only has your academic education been neglected, but your domestic training leaves a great deal to be desired. As for the rest, I have already pointed out to *you* that you are a Meandis, legally if not naturally, and as such you are my concern whether you like it or not.'

'But you can't——'

'Be silent!' Glittering dark eyes quelled her by the sheer force of the anger they suggested. But he was a man who knew how to control himself as well as others, and he brought his obviously formidable temper under control remarkably quickly. 'I believe you have made some attempt to remedy the domestic situation, and the academic loss is beyond redemption now, so we will say no more about it. But from now on you will be expected to do at least half the work in the house, and what you do not know you will learn under Aunt Alexia's guidance. You will start learning to become a useful member of society, my girl, and less of a butterfly! Do you understand?'

Bethany fumed. Her face was hot with colour and she clenched her hands tightly, and yet there was very little she could do at the moment. She would fare very badly if she was foolish enough to take herself off, as she had first threatened to do, for she had little ability for earning her own living. Looking across at Nikolas, she angled her chin and glared in futile resentment, but she did the only thing she could do at present.

With a short jerky nod of her head, she accepted his ruling. 'Yes,' she said, 'I understand perfectly!'

He held her reluctant gaze for several seconds, then nodded, and she thought his tight lips relaxed just a little. 'Good,' he approved. 'I'm sure we shall get along much better now that we understand one another.' Bethany said nothing, but she doubted it very much. 'Now,' said Nikolas, giving his attention to the papers in front of him, 'we come to matters that concern you both to some extent.'

'Papa's will,' Bethany dared to guess, for she recognised her stepfather's handwriting on the document at the top of the pile, and the heading was plain enough to see.

Nikolas nodded agreement and said nothing about her interruption. 'As you know, my cousin, poor Pavlos, had very little to leave in the way of worldly goods, but what little he had is left to Takis for the most part, not unnaturally, and to—his family in Rodos.' Bethany's head jerked up quickly and her eyes widened in disbelief, for she could not believe that Papa had ignored her completely. 'The contents of the studio go to Aunt Alexia to keep or dispose of as she prefers, and this house comes to you, Bethany, to be your dowry, as is the custom.'

The traditional dowry of the Greek bride, Bethany realised, and appreciated the honour it did her even while a curious little chill trickled through her veins. She looked at Nikolas warily, seeking his reassurance and not even stopping to think that he was the last person she would have expected to turn to.

'He didn't——' She passed the moistening tip of her tongue anxiously over dry lips. 'There's no mention of anyone—I mean, he didn't mention——'

'The man he wishes you to marry?' Nikolas enquired, so matter-of-factly that she felt a strange curling sensation in her stomach suddenly. 'It isn't written down, Bethany, but I know his wishes in the matter and if it's at all possible I shall see that they're complied with.'

'*No!*' She was on her feet, the dilapidated chair falling with a crash behind her as she faced him across the little makeshift desk. 'You know how I feel about arranged marriages, Nikolas, and you said you understood! I won't be—be handed over to just anyone you choose and spend the rest of my life standing at a kitchen sink and working like a slave for some man I don't even like! Even you wouldn't be so unfeeling as to force me into that!'

'If I fail to comply with my cousin's wishes,' Nikolas interrupted firmly, 'it will be because I would think twice about joining any man for life to a spoiled and wilful young woman who would probably make his life a misery! Now will you sit down, Bethany, and let us get on with the rest of the business?'

'There *is* no other business as far as I'm concerned!' Bethany insisted. 'You have to promise me, Nikolas, that you won't—— Aunt Alex!' She turned to the old lady anxiously, her hands as well as her grey eyes appealing to her. 'Please, you won't let him do this, will you?'

Alexia sympathised, she guessed, but she had been brought up in the old way and she would see nothing wrong in a girl's future being settled for her. It was the way things had always been done; the way they were still done by a great many people, particularly in the islands where progress had been slower and old ways died harder. Also there was little she could do to influence her redoubtable nephew, Bethany knew that, and felt a taste of bitterness for the changing climate of her safe little world.

'Trust Niko, child,' Alexia advised gently, but Bethany shook her head vehemently.

'That's just it,' she cried despairingly. 'I *don't* trust him!'

'Be silent!' Nikolas said sharply. 'Pick up that chair, Bethany, and sit down, there is no need for hysteria.

You have my word that you will not be forced to marry anyone you are not quite willing to marry. Does that satisfy you?'

Still shaking with emotion, she faced him across the table, only now realising that he too had got to his feet, leaning his weight on his hands and bringing his dark, strong face close to hers. 'You mean it?'

Her voice shivered uncertainly and he drew a deep breath, coping with a rapidly thinning patience, she guessed. 'Trust me, as Aunt Alexia suggests. Is that so difficult to do?'

She shook her head, glancing from the corner of her eye at Alexia's encouraging expression. Without a word, she bent and picked up the chair, then sat down on it, holding her hands in her lap as she had been. Nikolas, once she was seated, resumed his own seat and sat for a moment running his long hands through the papers in front of him before he spoke.

'Shall we continue?' he asked, but Bethany heard little of what followed, for her own future loomed too largely in her mind for her to give much attention to anything else. And no matter what impression she had given, she still did not entirely trust him.

The situation proved less uncomfortable during the several days that followed than Bethany had feared, and so far she and Nikolas had had no really serious clash—possibly because she now did far more household chores than ever she had done before, and found it rather less irksome than she anticipated. Nikolas was tolerant to a degree, but he expected more of both her and Takis than Papa had ever done. And while Takis seemed quite amenable on the whole, yielding her accustomed freedom to Nikolas's determined discipline aroused both resentment and rebellion in Bethany.

With time to spare one day, she walked up the hill above the harbour to visit the artists' colony, returning windblown and warmly flushed, carrying her sandals as she continued barefoot along the quay. Going barefoot occasionally was something she had done since childhood, partly because she liked the feeling, and partly because it was something that a lot of the people from the art colony did.

It set them apart from the village people, made them different, and Bethany had inherited enough of her mother's character to enjoy being different sometimes. There was a spring in her step and she was smiling to herself as she walked past the fishing boats moored in bobbing rows all along the harbour wall, pleased because she thought she had eluded Nikolas's eagle eye for once.

'*Aie!* Will you look over here!'

The half-mocking voice turned to chuckles, joined by others; deep, friendly laughter from the young men working in the boats, but Bethany was so accustomed to them by now that she did no more than smile to herself as she walked on. Whistles and catcalls shrilled among the laughter, and she knew that if she so much as turned her head and looked at one of them he would immediately become the target of his friends' teasing, mocking his prowess with women. It was all harmless enough, and it had never troubled her at all.

It was different on this occasion, however, for Nikolas was standing along at the end of the quay beside his own boat, and he waited for her to come along, with a look that spoke volumes. As if they had only just noticed him and realised his mood, her admirers returned to their tasks with merely a wry grin among themselves, while Bethany was obliged to face the dark censorious eyes that noted her bare feet and disapproved.

She was already on the defensive when she stopped beside him, and she put a hand on his arm to balance herself while she slipped her feet into her sandals. 'I've walked barefoot before, Nikolas,' she told him. 'It doesn't hurt when you're hardened to it.'

When they moved on, Nikolas made sure that she walked just slightly ahead of him, so that their progress along the narrow path from the quay suggested he was herding her and preventing her escape. 'Are you also hardened to the remarks of the men who whistle and call after you?' he asked, and Bethany turned and looked at him over her shoulder, the colour in her cheeks deepening slightly.

'They do no harm,' she told him, but had little hope of convincing him. 'It's only fun, Nikolas.'

'Fun!' He spoke harshly and caught her arm, pulling her round to face him now that they were out of sight of the quay and for the moment unobserved. The narrow, stony road curved around a garden wall and a straggling plane tree cast a shadow over them that turned Nikolas's eyes to jet-black. 'What kind of a woman do you think they consider you, Bethany? Your hair blown into a tangle and your feet bare, flushed and smiling—— Mother of God, but you show yourself off like a whore!'

'How *dare* you say such things to me!' She faced him with bright, indignant grey eyes, and she was trembling with anger. 'And you sound very familiar with the subject; maybe *you're* not as virtuous as you try to sound!'

'You——' His eyes blazed and, seeing them, she cringed inwardly, for he had seldom appeared more awe-inspiring than at that moment. But while she watched him with awed fascination, he was already bringing his formidable temper under control. 'Not only are you wanton in your looks, but you have the undisciplined insolence of a street-urchin,' he informed her relentlessly. 'You are a Meandis, whether or not you choose to remember it, and you will *not* walk about the village looking as you do, or smiling at every man you pass, as if you enjoy the sensation you cause. Do you understand me?'

'I won't be bullied, Nikolas!' Her breathing was short and uneven, and lurking not too far behind the anger were tears. She tried so hard to get along with him, she told herself, but still he found fault, and she despaired of their ever understanding one another. Looking up at him, she shook her head. 'Oh, why don't you go away and leave me alone?' she whispered. 'I was happy until you came, and now——'

'Now that you're being made to grow up and behave like a woman instead of a wanton child, you resent it!' His eyes gleamed darkly in the shadow of the plane tree, but there was a very faint suggestion of softening in the firm line of his mouth as he looked down at her. 'I realise how hard it must be for you, Bethany, but you must have realised that one day all this—this butterfly existence would have to come to an end. Didn't you?'

Bethany didn't answer for several moments because she could not find the words; she simply stood looking down at the vee of bronzed skin where his shirt opened, and tried to think of ways she could earn her own living. She was a modest sculptor and a fairly good painter, but there were so many in Greece already, and she had no other talents. For all his harshness and his curtailment of her freedom, Nikolas offered a curiously comforting kind of security, and she didn't want to leave Apolidus, or Aunt Alexia and Takis.

'Papa never found anything wrong with my walking about barefoot,' she told him, and Nikolas shook his head, but there was a kind of gentleness in his voice just the same that she noted and clung to hopefully.

'Your papa spoiled you,' he said, 'and now *I* must make of you what I can; it isn't an easy task.'

Glancing upward, she caught his eye for just a second. 'What *are* you trying to make of me, Nikolas?' she asked.

He did not answer at once, and eventually she once more looked up at the dark, brooding eyes beneath their black lashes. 'I'm trying to make a mortal of you,' he said softly, after a moment or two. 'You live too much in your own world, Bethany, and somehow I have to make a normal flesh and blood woman of you —a Meandis for preference.'

She stirred, curiously uneasy suddenly, the colour in her cheeks more evident again. 'Does it matter?' she asked. 'I doubt if you'll be able to change me now.'

Nikolas reached out and took a handful of bright tawny hair, holding it so tightly that she felt the pull of his strong fingers at her scalp. Looking down into her face while he held back her head, he gazed for a long, silent moment at her mouth. 'Perhaps not,' he said with unexpected candour, and let her hair run through his fingers as he released her. 'Come,' he added, turning her about, 'Aunt Alexia will need your help with dinner.'

Alexia's support of Nikolas when she heard about their verbal skirmish, brought home to Bethany the fact that there were some aspects of Pavlos's lenient upbringing that Alexia frowned upon almost as disapprovingly as Nikolas did. She probably always had in her heart, but she was a kindly woman and had a genuine love for her nephew by marriage and his family. Under Nikolas's more strict authority, however, she probably saw less need to conceal her own more traditional views.

She had always been concerned, she confessed to Bethany, that she took such little care with her reputation, and she wished Bethany would believe that Nikolas had only her best interests at heart. Bethany's retort that she doubted very much if Nikolas had a heart brought a gently reproachful frown. He was very concerned about her, Alexia insisted.

Takis was wildly excited a couple of days later when Nikolas anounced that he had arranged for them to take a trip to Rhodes so that he and Bethany could meet more of the Meandis family. Bethany's reaction was less enthusiastic, a point that Nikolas did not fail to notice and remark on.

'I see no reason why you behave as if I'm sending you into exile,' Nikolas told her impatiently. 'You're simply going on a visit to other members of the family, and you'll be welcomed, you need have no fear of that.' His dark eyes quizzed her shrewdly for a moment. 'Is that what bothers you, Bethany? That you won't be welcome because you're Pavlos's adopted child rather than his natural one?'

His constant reference to her as a child always irritated Bethany, but she let it go in this instance while she considered the reason for her reluctance to accompany him on the trip. 'I just thought——' She shrugged, reluctant to put it into words. 'I can't help feeling that you won't be the only one of your family who views me with a disapproving eye,' she told him. 'And it won't be much of a pleasure trip if I have to spend the whole time watching every word I say and every move I make.'

'Do you do that here?' he countered with surprising mildness, and she looked at him as if he was being rather obtuse.

'You know I do, ever since you came, Nikolas. And it's bad enough here, but among a lot of strangers——'

'Your family,' Nikolas insisted firmly, but a faint smile touched the firm lines of his mouth for a moment. 'And I hope you won't make such dramatic claims about having to watch every word, etcetera, to the family, Bethany, or you'll have them thinking I've turned into some kind of tyrannical monster since I came here.'

'I didn't say anything of the kind,' Bethany objected, but Nikolas was shaking his head slowly.

'You don't have to when you look so woebegone. My reputation will be ruined if you continue to look so soulful and unhappy.'

'Do I?' It hadn't occurred to her that she gave quite that impression, and she looked at him curiously. 'Do I really look soulful and unhappy, Nikolas?'

'Sometimes,' Nikolas insisted, and that slight smile still lingered about his mouth. 'I'm not really such a brute, am I, Bethany?' She shook her head rather than condemn him that fiercely, and he went on. 'I'm simply trying to make a woman of you.'

Urged on by heaven knew what, Bethany glanced upward, and her mouth was softly appealing, her lips slightly parted with a suggestion of guileless innocence. 'And is being a woman only a matter of cooking and cleaning, and never walking barefoot along the quay, or laughing at the way the fishermen talk? Isn't there something more to it than that, Nikolas?'

If she had but known it there was the look of her mother about the way she glanced at him, and his mouth tightened ominously, banishing the smile altogether. 'Holy Mother!' he breathed with pious softness. 'You can't mean to be as provoking as you look!'

'I only meant that if you're teaching me, Nikolas, shouldn't you——'

'Be still!' Nikolas commanded firmly, but there was a certain look in his eyes that belied the sternness of his tone and sent a shivering little thrill of excitement running through her veins. 'You'll go to Rodos with us, and you'll behave like a civilised young woman or you'll answer to me, my girl! You won't behave as if you're a poor little orphan bullied by her guardian, nor will you flaunt yourself before every man you see! And if you so much as look at——'

He stopped short and shook his head, but again that thrilling sense of exhilaration possessed her, egging her on. 'Who mustn't I look at, Nikolas?' she asked meekly.

Nikolas ran his long fingers through his hair and half turned from her. 'Go and help Alexia,' he ordered sternly, 'and don't ever try to provoke me too far, Bethany, or you'll find out just how much of a tyrant I *can* be!'

'Nikolas——'

'Go!' he insisted harshly, and she turned swiftly, a bright warm colour in her cheeks.

But resentful as she was at being ordered so harshly, there was nevertheless a curious thrill of elation stirring in Bethany's blood as she obeyed him. It was a strange feeling to realise she had the power to push Nikolas to the point of losing that iron self-control of his, and it was a sensation she had to admit she enjoyed, although she wasn't sure she understood it.

Alexia was quite frank about her feelings. She

looked forward to the trip to Rhodes as excitedly as
Takis did, and only Bethany was at all reluctant to go.
It brought home to her, too, that for the first time in
her life she was disturbingly at odds with the two
people, next to Papa, who had always meant most in
the world to her. It troubled her and she sought
reasons for it.

In part she attributed it to the reasons she had given
Nikolas, but it was also because she had always had
an aversion to change, especially when it meant leaving Apolidus. It was a feeling that probably stemmed
from those restless years of wandering when, as a tiny
child, she had been moved from one commune to another without ever being quite sure who her parents
were, or where she belonged. In Apolidus she felt
secure as she never had anywhere else.

If she could have managed to elude Nikolas she
would have stayed behind, even at the very last minute, when she came downstairs wearing a demurely
pretty blue print dress that was at least two years old.
She wore her hair loose and it had been brushed until it gleamed like burnished bronze, and she looked
much less than her eighteen years.

She found Nikolas alone when she came down into
the living-room, and something about the way he
smiled faintly when he first caught sight of her put her
immediately on the defensive. 'I suppose you think
this dress a bit—ordinary for visiting rich relations,'
she guessed, rashly aggressive because she suspected he
was laughing at her very everyday little dress. 'We
don't have the latest fashions here, you know, and you
didn't expect me to wear my Sunday black, did you?'

'We can do something about buying you more
clothes when we get to Rodos,' Nikolas told her. 'In the
meantime you have no need to feel you're the poor relation, Bethany.' He arched a black brow at her quizzi-
cally. 'That was behind your outburst, wasn't it?'

'I suppose so.' She avoided his eyes carefully when
she answered. 'I thought perhaps you found my
dress——'

'It's very pretty and it suits you,' Nikolas told her, and the pitch of his voice was subtly different somehow, so that the colour warming her cheeks was something she couldn't help. 'You look very young, Bethany; it's very hard to believe you're eighteen. You remind me of my first sight of you, nearly four years ago —a beautiful child, coming up to womanhood.'

Compliments like Nikolas paid her were a completely new experience, and affected her much more deeply than the bold whistles and laughter of the village youths. They could be laughed off, but somehow it was not possible to suspect him of being merely flighty. Stroking a hand over her hair, tawny in the sunlight from the window, she did her best to cope.

'You didn't think much of me on that occasion,' she reminded him, then laughed unsteadily. 'I suppose that hasn't changed much either, has it, Nikolas?'

He had taken over Pavlos's old and overstuffed armchair, and he leaned back against the shabby cushions, completely at ease. His long legs crossed and his hands on the chair arms, he watched her where she stood in the sunlit window, and the shadows in the big room moulded curves and angles into his ruggedly handsome features, giving prominence to high cheekbones and a deeply cleft chin, making smudged shadows of the thick lashes hiding his slightly almond-shaped eyes.

'Did it trouble you that I disapproved, Bethany?' he asked quietly, and she turned away from him uneasily, into the full sun, closing her eyes for a moment against its brilliance. 'Does it still trouble you?'

'Not as much as it did.' She didn't bother to deny that it had troubled her, or that it still did, for he had not really needed to ask. 'I hated you,' she added without turning her head, and she heard him click his tongue in the expression of impatience she was fast becoming familiar with. Turning to look over her shoulder, she angled her chin in defiance of his impatience. 'You don't believe it?' she challenged.

'I find it unreasonable!'

'Do you?' She turned back to the window, a thudding pulse at her temple warning her that she was treading on dangerous ground. 'I'm not sure I've changed either, Nikolas.'

He swore, but the oath was too muffled for her to recognise it, then he got up out of Pavlos's chair, coming to stand immediately behind her so that she felt suddenly trapped. His nearness brought unexpected warmth to her flesh through the thin cotton dress, and yet she felt herself shiver.

'You're stubborn!'

'To add to my other sins!' Bethany retorted quickly before he could go on, and he gripped her shoulder, spinning her round to face him, so that she could see the glittering darkness of his eyes at close quarters.

His fingers dug deep and hurt, and she tried to shrug him off, grasping his wrist with her slim fingers. 'I ought to——' He let her go suddenly and turned swiftly away, running one hand over the back of his head in a gesture that was tauntingly reminiscent of Papa. 'Go and see where Takis has got to.' His voice was once more firmly under control, brisk and confident. 'I thought he at least was anxious to meet his cousins.'

Bethany looked up at him and was surprised to realise how much she regretted being the one who had changed the mood from compliments to recriminations. 'I know he is,' she assured him.

His hand on her shoulder stopped her before she moved away, and she looked up at him with slightly apprehensive grey eyes. 'None of the family have seen Pavlos for—a great many years,' said Nikolas, and Bethany had the impression he was choosing his words very carefully. 'He loved you and Takis, he loved you both very deeply, and how they think of Pavlos depends quite a lot on how you and Takis impress them, try and remember that, Bethany. You're his—his vindication.'

'His vindication?' His choice of term puzzled her and she frowned up at him curiously.

Nikolas considered for a moment, and she could not

imagine what was going on behind those deeply serious eyes, but she was trembling and her legs felt horribly unsteady. 'There are things you don't know, child,' he said after a moment or two, and she once more resented that unwelcome terminology but said nothing about it.

'Papa did nothing to be ashamed of,' she declared in a small and not very steady voice, for somehow she felt she was speaking with less than her usual certainty when she spoke of Papa, and it troubled her. 'We hadn't much money, but we were happy and he always——' She broke off and caught her bottom lip between small sharp white teeth as she shook her head slowly. 'You don't know what it was like here then, Nikolas.'

He said nothing for a moment, but his hand still rested on her shoulder and Bethany could not simply walk away from him in that event. Then he used the same hand to stroke one long forefinger lightly down her cheek and there was a warmth in his eyes again. 'I can guess,' he said softly, and Bethany's heart beat with a breathtaking urgency suddenly. 'Now go and find Takis, will you, Bethany? It's time we were leaving.'

'You wouldn't let me——'

'I wouldn't dream of leaving you here,' Nikolas affirmed quietly, and Bethany turned quickly and went to do as he said, feeling oddly satisfied that he had answered as he did, but not in the least understanding her own reaction.

# CHAPTER THREE

THERE was something undeniably thrilling about skimming across the blue Aegean in the motor launch that Nikolas handled with such skill and panache, and the effect was to make Bethany feel slightly less apprehensive about the coming visit for the moment. The yielding surface of the ocean was like a silken cushion shedding white feathers in their wake that were tossed and fluttered by a playful wind.

The trip was taking rather longer than Bethany anticipated, but she knew it was quite a distance to the largest of the Dodecanese islands; Rhodes was quite close to the coast of Turkey. It was a journey broken by a seemingly endless scattering of small islands spread out between the mainlands of the two countries, and each one with its own exotic place in mythology.

The sun was hot and dazzling on the water, but a cooling wind made it bearable, and for the moment Bethany stood in the cockpit of the boat with Nikolas and Takis. 'How much further is it, Nikolas?' she asked, and he turned his head and eyed her for a moment before he answered her.

'Not much further now,' he promised. 'Don't you enjoy boats, Bethany?'

'Oh yes!' She considered how far they had come and something about the way Takis was looking struck her as vaguely suspicious; it made her uneasy and she wondered why. 'It just seems rather a long trip to make in one day, that's all.'

Nikolas was not looking at her any longer, but he spoke in the same quiet and matter-of-fact tone as before. 'I don't remember saying it was a day trip,' he remarked, and Bethany stared at him, too stunned for a moment to say anything.

Takis seemed to find her reaction very amusing, and

hazily Bethany registered the fact that their once mutual tastes seemed to have diverged lately. 'We're going for several days,' he informed her with obvious relish. 'Didn't you know, Beth?'

Bethany sat down very suddenly on the narrow seat inside the cockpit, for her legs no longer felt capable of supporting her, and she was half deafened by the thudding beat of her heart as she contemplated what was in store for her. For the moment she could only think that Nikolas meant them never to return to Apolidus, and at the thought of that her whole being rebelled.

'You had no right,' she whispered, her voice barely audible above the hum of the engine, and Nikolas regarded her with raised brows. 'Why, Nikolas?' She looked down at the simple blue dress and spread her hands in a gesture of helpless frustration because she knew why he had not told her, and given her time to argue against the trip even more earnestly. 'Do you realise that this is all I have with me?' she asked bitterly.

Takis was obviously puzzled by her objections, but Nikolas could hardly claim to be surprised by them. Nevertheless he looked as if he saw her protest not only as inevitable but too unimportant to arouse anything more in him than a faint irritation. 'All that will be taken care of when we arrive,' he explained in a firmly controlled voice. 'You'll go with Aunt Alexia and buy whatever you need; her word will be the final one on whatever you choose, but you may be quite lavish in the circumstances.'

'In compensation!' Bethany guessed, and sat restlessly twining her fingers together. She felt resentful and oddly deflated, because he had made it difficult for her to express her anger as forthrightly as she would have done in other circumstances. 'Must you treat me like a baby, Nikolas?'

The long brown hands on the wheel tightened perceptibly, and she noticed Takis's swift sideways glance that anticipated a lash of temper. Instead he spoke quietly, but in a voice that was very obviously under strong restraint. 'Takis,' he said, 'will you go below and see how Aunt Alexia is doing?'

Rather than risk the anger lurking in the dark eyes, bursting upon him, Takis did as he said, but it was clear he would rather have stayed and seen the outcome. Nikolas waited until he had ducked down the narrow companionway into the small neat cabin, then he turned on Bethany and gave the fury in his eyes full rein.

'I've been patient to the point of idiocy with you,' he said in a flat hard voice, 'but if you behave like a spoiled child and ruin this visit, Bethany, I'll deal with you as Pavlos should have done years ago! Do you understand me?'

'You should have told me!' Bethany insisted, and in her frustration the words almost choked her. 'Why didn't you tell me as you did Takis? Is it this—this male superiority thing you're so keen on? I'm a woman so I don't have to be told anything, even if it concerns me intimately! Did Aunt Alex know she was being brought here for—for heaven knows how long?'

'Aunt Alexia thought you'd worry about it if you knew too soon,' he told her, obviously very reluctant to admit that the idea had not been his alone. 'You apparently hate leaving your precious island for any reason at all, and rather than have you fretting about it, or even finding reasons why you couldn't come with us, we didn't tell you. The matter of luggage didn't arise because, as I've already said, you and Takis are to be fitted out completely when we get to Rodos.'

Her lip refused to stop trembling and tears were already running down her cheeks, and yet she could not really think of any reason for her weeping, except that she had been fooled, and that for the very best of reasons. Getting up, she would have gone to stand in the stern of the boat, but before she could pass him Nikolas put a hand on the edge of the cockpit and blocked her way.

She stood for a moment, stiff as a statue and shivering inwardly as if she was afraid of something nameless that threatened her precious security. Then she looked up at Nikolas's dark, stern face and found it oddly reassuring. 'Let me go,' she pleaded in a small and not very steady voice. 'I—I'd like to stand in the stern and—and watch the way the—the way the water curves away.'

Still that long arm blocked her way, and ducking underneath it did not even occur to her. 'It's out of sight, Bethany,' he said quietly, and she shook her head, denying that she had been going to see if Apolidus was still in sight. 'This is the first step, why don't you enjoy it? There are people waiting to welcome you and you'll love Rodos almost as much as you do Apolidus.' His mouth curved upward at the corners into a smile that showed in the depth of his eyes too, and he let down his arms at last. 'You'll enjoy buying new clothes too, won't you?'

She nodded. There was something incredibly persuasive about that deep soft voice, even in the flattening dullness of the open air, and she *would* enjoy buying a whole new wardrobe, she could not deny it. It was the first opportunity she had ever had of being so extravagant and she was, after all, a perfectly normal eighteen-year-old in that respect.

'It's—it's very good of you, Nikolas,' she said in a small and rather choked voice. 'I'm—I'm sorry about——'

He placed the back of one hand against her bare arm and stroked the long fingers downward very slowly, sending curious little shivers through her whole being. 'I can't guarantee that Rodos has *all* the latest fashions,' he said, 'but I'm sure you'll find something to suit you.'

Trembling slightly and more affected by that rare contact with him than she cared to admit, she tried to thank him. 'I'm sure I will, thank you, Nikolas.' It was purely impulse that made her stand on tiptoe suddenly and kiss his smooth brown cheek lightly be-

fore she turned away, but it seemed to Bethany that he
too half turned his head and put his lips briefly against
her cheek.

The moment she appeared below, Takis eyed her
narrowly and with some disappointment, she thought,
when it became obvious she had not cried hard enough
or long enough for it to show. Then he disappeared on
deck again, and left Bethany to make rather desultory
conversation with Aunt Alexia. The old lady, she felt,
was curiously absent in her manner, although there
was no doubt at all that she looked forward to this visit
with nothing but pleasure. Neither of them mentioned
her being deceived.

Bethany was once more on deck with Takis and
Nikolas when they got their first sight of the island of
Rhodes, and she felt other feelings than simply appre-
hension mingling in her wildly beating heart as she
watched it grow ever closer. The city of the same name
was at the far north-eastern end of the island, and
within sight of the Turkish mainland, and it was for
there that they were making.

The entrance to Rhodes harbour came into sight,
with its stone columns supporting huge sculpted deer;
the stag at one side and the doe at the other. And the
ancient windmills strung along the breakwater that
formed one side of the harbour looked squat and enduring with their scrawny sails turning lazily against
the background of blue sky; enduring as Rhodes itself.

With Nikolas's reassurances in mind, there was no
reason why she felt as she did, but the nearer they got
to their mooring, the worse that niggling sense of ap-
prehension. Soon she would meet Pavlos's other family
and be judged. Nikolas took them in through the harbour entrance by the domes and arches of the new
Market, overshadowed by the soaring towers and ram-
parts of the Knights' Town, built and held by the
Knights of St John for more than two hundred years.
The inner harbour was crowded, but somehow the
motor cruiser was fitted into a berth, and Bethany
held tightly to Nikolas's hand as he helped her ashore,

for her legs were trembling as well as her hands.

Nothing, of course, was left to chance, Nikolas Meandis was not that sort of man, and a car was waiting for them—a huge luxurious German model attended by a tall young man who came hurrying over to meet them, and over whose presence Nikolas was frowning even before he spoke. He was no hired man, that was obvious, for he had a bouncing self-confidence as well as good looks, and Bethany glanced curiously at Nikolas.

With a beamingly impudent smile the young man gathered Aunt Alexia in to his embrace and kissed her heartily on both cheeks. 'Aunt Alex! Oh, why have you been away so long? We're all so glad you're back and we shall never let you out of our sight again! Welcome, welcome, dear aunt!'

His boisterous good humour acted as a reviver for Bethany's low spirits, and she was smiling without being aware of doing so, until the bright dark eyes were turned on her. He sent his gaze skimming over her from head to toe in such obvious appreciation that she felt herself colouring furiously, then he pursed his lips in a silent whistle and shook his head.

He would, Bethany suspected, have introduced himself had Nikolas not intervened first. A rather surprisingly possessive hand was slipped under her elbow and drew her forward slightly. 'Bethany, this is my brother Theodore; Theo, Bethany Meandis, the adopted daughter of our cousin Pavlos.'

All very precise and accurate, Bethany noted. It designated her position exactly as an acquired member of the family rather than a born one, and she wondered if that slight difference was to be stressed by others before the day was out. But whatever Nikolas's opinion, it was quite clear that Theo Meandis had no reservations at all. Her hand was taken and squeezed firmly, then, before she could prepare herself for it, she was pulled into an embrace as bold and enthusiastic as that he had given Alexia. He kissed her on both cheeks too, as he had Alexia, but with a subtle difference.

His lips were warm and smooth and they lingered over-long on her soft cool skin, then he looked directly down into her eyes, boldly seeking her reaction while he spoke. 'Welcome, cousin,' he murmured, then laughed. 'Had *I* found you hidden away on a quiet little island I'd have kept you there for myself! But then that is Nikolas for you, eh?'

Overwhelmed, Bethany said nothing and it was Nikolas who once more took over the conversation. 'I asked that Petrakis bring the car to meet us,' he reminded his brother, and was obviously annoyed because his instructions had been countermanded.

But Theodore Meandis merely shrugged, thrusting out his lower lip. 'I came instead,' he told him, stating the obvious. 'It makes no difference, surely, Niko.'

'It means that instead of Takis and me shopping by taxi and Aunt Alex and Bethany having the use of the car,' Nikolas pointed out with barely contained impatience, 'the ladies will now have to use a taxi while we take the car, since they are without a driver.'

'*I'm* a driver,' Theo reminded him, and caught Bethany's hastily lowered eyes. 'And I'm quite willing to drive the ladies anywhere they wish to go.'

'I have no doubt,' Nikolas replied dryly, 'but you'll come with me, Theo, and leave Aunt Alexia and Bethany to do their own shopping. It isn't something you can help with, and I'm sure the shopping will take much less time if you're not—helping.'

'Niko——'

'Please find a taxi,' Nikolas told him, ignoring his attempted pleas, and it was no real surprise when the younger brother obeyed with little more than a resigned shrug.

For all that, he half turned his head as he went and once more caught Bethany's eye and, while he did not actually wink, he came very close to it, so that she automatically smiled to herself. Rather than encourage him further, however, she appeared to take a passing interest in what was going on around her and, quite unexpectedly, found herself under scrutiny from another source.

It was probably quite coincidental, of course, but it seemed as if someone standing over near the New Market had been watching her quite intently until she caught his eye. A man, standing near one of the arched entrances to the market, wearing a light suit and with nothing on his head so that she had a really good look at his face, considering the distance between them.

He was tall and lean, as far as she could judge, and evidently unwilling to have it realised that he was watching her, for he looked away and moved off the moment she made it obvious she had seen him. Hands thrust into his pockets and his head averted, he went striding off and was soon lost among the crowds, but something about him made Bethany frown—some nagging, irresistible sense of familiarity that just for those few seconds had almost become recognition.

'Is something wrong?'

Inevitably it was Nikolas who asked, and Bethany shook her head quickly, for already the man's face was fading from her mind, and she thought he was probably just one of the artists she had seen at the commune in Apolidus anyway. 'Nothing's wrong,' she assured Nikolas, but she noticed that his eyes narrowed slightly as if he was not altogether sure she was being honest.

'You'll find it easier shopping without Theo,' he promised, and from his expression he was not being facetious about it. He consulted the watch encircling his wrist, then looked at his aunt. 'Shall we expect you in about two hours, Aunt Alexia?' he suggested, and having got Alexia's assent, he gave his attention to Bethany once more, surprising her with a show of gentleness in his eyes for a moment. 'I know you'll enjoy yourself, little one,' he told her, using an endearment he had never used before and which his brother marked with a swiftly elevated brow. 'But not too extravagantly, eh?'

'Oh no, of course not,' she assured him, and could not help wondering why it was that when he smiled as

he did then, it was so hard to remember how much she
hated him sometimes.

'In two hours,' he reminded them, and added the
ancient blessing. 'Be happy!'

It was at Alexia's suggestion that she kept on one of her
new dresses, but Bethany suspected that the idea might
have been Nikolas's. He knew how limited her wardrobe was, and she had left him in little doubt that she
did not like the idea of meeting the more wealthy members of the family dressed as she had arrived, in that
simple blue cotton dress.

If Nikolas had planned it this way so that she and
Takis need not appear looking like poor relations,
then she owed him thanks for his thoughtfulness, for
she certainly felt more up to the occasion decked out
in her new clothes. Alexia, presumably under Nikolas's direction, had encouraged her to buy not only
dresses but shoes and the most exquisite silk lingerie
as well, and when she saw herself in a dress-shop mir-
ror, Bethany even felt like a different person.

For the moment the question of how much money
had been spent caused no more than an occasional
niggle at the back of her mind, but sitting in a taxi
some time later, the question became more immediate
and she hoped Nikolas wasn't going to think she had
been too extravagant, and taken advantage of the situation. Whatever other qualities he brought to his role
of guardian, he had proved generous, and she was
ready to give him his due, but she would have been
happier knowing what else he had in store for her.

Alexia had told her that the Meandis home was in
New Rodos, but in fact the area proved to be not
strictly new at all. The houses were old, but gracious
in their age and surrounded by beautiful gardens behind high walls that jealously guarded the privacy of
the residents. Quite different from modern Rhodes
which sprawled its square box houses all over the hill-
sides and along the coast; white and dazzling like sugar
lumps in the sun.

From Alexia's expression it was clear that she was
happy to be coming home, and for a moment Bethany
felt curiously out of touch; as she had once or twice
lately. If Bethany had been coming in to Apolidus
she would have felt much the same as the old lady did,
she knew, but somehow, no matter how unreasonable
it might be, it hurt that Alexia was so obviously pleased
to have left it.

'Isn't it wonderful?' Alexia asked as they drove along
a delightfully tree-shaded street between high garden
walls, and seeing her bright and eager expression,
Bethany could do no other than agree.

'It's lovely,' she said, wishing she could face the coming situation with even a little of Alexia's happy anticipation.

'Oh, Bethany my child!' Alexia's light fingers pressed
over hers for a moment, seeking to reassure her. 'You
have nothing to fear, and you look so lovely in that
beautiful dress that everyone will love you on sight.
That deep turquoise colour suits you so perfectly.' She
turned quickly when the taxi drew up, and scarcely
gave the driver time to open the door for them. 'Come,
child, we're here!'

Like most of the other houses, the Meandis home
was built behind a high protective wall, and the garden beyond took Bethany's breath away. There were
masses of flowering trees and shrubs, scented and bril-
liant, shading ornamental paths of coloured pebbles
that wound their way towards a large house that sat,
almost smugly perfect, behind a screen of blood-red
rhododendrons. It was lush, extravagant and stagger-
ingly beautiful.

For a few seconds only the sweet trill of bird-song ac-
companied their footsteps along the pebble path, but
they had taken no more than a step or two when Theodore Meandis came hurrying along to meet them. His
dark eyes gleamed with pleasure at the sight of Bethany in the turquoise dress, and he beamed her a smile
that was irresistible.

'Aunt Alex! Bethany!'

His welcome was as enthusiastic as if he had not met them only a couple of hours ago on the quay, and he embraced and kissed them both with the same effusiveness as before. Perhaps with more fervour than before, for his hands rested heavily on Bethany's slim waist while he kissed her. Then with a hand under Alexia's arm he walked between them, his other hand reaching for and holding Bethany's, his firm fingers squeezing lightly.

'Welcome, lovely cousin,' he whispered, and very briefly lowered one eyelid. 'Nikolas believes you are too shy to meet us all at once, but Aunt Helen and Uncle Gregori are here, of course, and Mama, naturally.'

Bethany had no idea why he pulled a face when he mentioned his mother, but it did little to make her feel confident. She knew nothing about them at all, she realised as Theo took them in through a half-open door, and too late she wished she had asked Aunt Alexia. The trip had been sprung on her so unexpectedly that she had had no time to adjust to the idea at all, and she could only hope that some of the Meandises at least could be like Theo rather than Nikolas.

The house had looked big from the outside, inside it was overwhelming, and Bethany realised that her stepfather's background was far more impressive than she had ever realised. Even the hall seemed huge, and before Theo whisked them across it at speed, she had time to notice wide carpeted stairs decorated with brass lamps on the newel posts, and a blue and white tiled floor that ricocheted their combined footsteps like gunfire from the plain cool walls.

A door opened and Theo ushered them into a big airy drawing-room, carpeted and elegantly furnished, but unexpectedly ornate and with a suggestion of the Orient about it—red Turkish carpet on the floor, and furniture that was old looking and comfortable, deep-seated chairs with enormous cushions, and small tables with inlaid tops or enormous brass trays in lieu of a top.

The ceiling was high and shadowy, and the walls hung with ornately woven rugs and gilt-framed mirrors, while overhead, suspended from chains, were brass lamps ornately decorated and polished to the gleam of mirrors. She was vaguely aware of there being four or five people in the room, but it startled her to realise that she was thankful to see Nikolas come forward to greet them.

His eyes took immediate note of her dress, but it was impossible to judge his reaction to it. Takis, she just had time to notice, looked equally resplendent, though barely recognisable, in a smart blue suit with long trousers, and a white shirt, nothing like the little brother she was used to, running around in the briefest of shorts and a T-shirt.

'You've enjoyed yourself?' Nikolas asked, and Bethany nodded.

Alexia had left them, already being hugged back into the bosom of her family, and Nikolas caught Bethany's eyes as he took charge of the introductions. Theo yielded the task reluctantly, she thought, but he yielded nevertheless, and she once more marvelled at the kind of awe Nikolas Meandis could command, even in his own family.

'Don't look so much as if you're being served to the lions for supper,' Nikolas murmured, bending his head slightly to bring himself nearer. 'They are your family, Bethany, and no one's going to eat you!' Swiftly his eyes swept over her, noting the way the soft material of the dress clung and flattered her figure, then he shook his head. 'Possibly Aunt Alexia did not take into account the fact that you are not boyishly slim when she allowed you to have that dress,' he added, and Bethany felt the colour flood into her face as she prepared to defend her choice.

'I thought it suited me,' she whispered, aware that she was being scrutinised by at least one pair of eyes, and just for a second Nikolas's fingers tightened on her arm, as if in warning.

'It suits you perfectly,' he agreed in that disturbingly

quiet voice of his, 'but the effect is rather more—sultry
than is suitable for a young girl.' Bethany would have
protested more vehemently, but he had brought them
to a halt where an elderly woman sat in one of the
armchairs, watching them with hooded dark eyes.
'Mama,' he went on, still holding Bethany's arm as if
he feared she might run away, 'this is Bethany. Bethany, my mother, who you will know as Aunt Nurmina.'

While she took a long slim hand and shook it, Bethany took note of how much darker Nurmina Meandis
was than the rest of her family. The rather bony face
gave a first impression of being harsh, but after a second or two Bethany noticed that the eyes were warm
and kindly, even though she did not actually smile.

'A beautiful child,' she said, and surprised Bethany
by speaking Greek with a faint but definite accent of
some kind. Her surprise must have shown, for Kiría
Meandis reached out and patted her cheek lightly.
'You are puzzled, little one, eh?' She glanced at Nikolas with her gleaming dark eyes, then shook her head.
'I am Turkish, my child, did Niko not tell you so?'

'No, Kiría—Aunt Nurmina.'

It was not really so surprising, Bethany thought, for
mixed marriages were not unknown, and it certainly
accounted for that slightly Oriental look she had
noticed about Nikolas. It was much less apparent in
Theo, but then apart from a basic family likeness, the
two brothers were not really very much alike at all.

'You're eighteen, are you not?' Nurmina asked, and
Bethany nodded. It seemed that Nikolas got his penchant for asking questions in that curiously interrogative way from his mother, and not merely from his
legal training. 'Such a sweet age,' Nurmina went on,
and reached out to lift a strand of Bethany's tawny
hair, letting it run through her fingers as if its bright-
ness fascinated her. 'And you're so fair, child.'

'I'm English,' Bethany told her, aware that Nikolas
was frowning over the claim. 'I know Nikolas says I'm

Greek now, but you can't make someone into another nationality just by saying they are.'

Nurmina caught her son's eye and her own dark ones gleamed with amusement for a moment. 'Your pupil questions your teaching, Niko,' she told him, not without a certain amount of satisfaction, Bethany felt. 'You cannot have been very convincing.'

Once more Nikolas slid a hand beneath her arm and Bethany felt the squeeze of strong fingers into her flesh for a moment. 'I have a very stubborn pupil,' he told his mother, and drew Bethany aside. 'You'd better come and meet the others; if you will excuse us, Mama.'

It was irresistible, and Bethany turned her head as he led her away, catching once more that deep dark gleam in Nurmina Meandis's eyes. Whoever else she had to contend with, she felt sure she had made a friend and ally in Nikolas's mother, and already she felt better.

Nikolas's Aunt Helen and her husband, Gregori, had proved to be pleasant and kindly people and welcomed her, just as he had promised, with a genuine warmth, so that the meeting had proved far less of an ordeal than Bethany anticipated. It made it easier too, that the conversation that evening buzzed with reminiscences, so that all she had to do was sit and listen to what was going on around her.

They had only just finished breakfast the following morning when a young manservant brought the telephone outside and informed Nikolas that there was a call for him. Bethany was sitting next to him when he took the call and, judging by his expression, he found himself at something of a disadvantage. It seemed to Bethany that whatever the call concerned, he would have preferred to have taken it in private rather than with most of the household overhearing.

Her suspicion was confirmed when he put the receiver down a few minutes later. 'Heracles,' he said briefly, in response to his mother's questioning look, and she nodded. 'He's impatient and would like us to go over this morning, as soon as possible.'

'It is natural, my son,' Nurmina Meandis said in her soft deep voice, and just for a moment her dark eyes strayed towards Bethany. 'You will all go, of course?'

'Of course,' Nikolas agreed, though it was obvious that whatever action the telephone call had precipitated he would have preferred to delay. 'I had thought perhaps—tomorrow——'

He shook his head, as if his own caution irritated him, and his mother looked at him with her deep dark eyes across the width of the table. 'It isn't possible, Niko,' she insisted. 'It must be now, if Heracles has asked for it; how could you refuse?'

'I can't, of course.' Nevertheless it was obvious he was disturbed in no small way by whatever the call concerned, and it was so unusual to see Nikolas having to do something he would rather not have done that Bethany watched him with more intensity than she realised—so intently that he was bound to sense it sooner or later, and when he looked up suddenly and caught her eye, he held her slightly uncertain gaze steadily as if he was still trying to determine his course of action. 'Bethany——'

He was so long before he said anything else that she looked at him curiously. 'What is it, Nikolas?'

'We're going to visit—other members of the family,' he told her, as if her gentle prompt had given him the spur he needed. 'You, Takis and Aunt Alexia, if she will.' His aunt had been involved in an animated conversation with Helen and Gregori, but she looked up when she heard her name and was obviously unaware of anything untoward until she noticed Nikolas's face. 'That was Heracles on the phone,' Nikolas explained, and it was impossible to miss the way Alexia caught her bottom lip between her teeth suddenly. 'He would like us to drive over there this morning, Aunt; will you come with us?'

Just briefly Alexia's soft dark eyes touched on Bethany, then she nodded. 'Yes, of course I will, Niko.'

The quiet voice was as gentle as ever, but there was

something in her eyes that Bethany thought she had never seen there before, and she found it hard to believe that Alexia viewed the coming visit with consternation. Nevertheless when they set out in Nikolas's car less than half an hour later, the same slightly apprehensive look still lingered in her eyes, and it did nothing to encourage Bethany, who sat beside her in the back.

Unlike the family house in new Rhodes, the one they sought this morning was a large and ultra-modern one, glistening white with that sugar-cube look. It was traditional in as far as it was surrounded by a wall and a garden that overflowed with flowering shrubs and trees, and they had no sooner set foot in it than two small boys came running to meet them, flinging their arms around Nikolas's long legs in welcome.

He was obviously a popular visitor and the two tiny welcomers clung to him tightly, chattering both at once and laughing, arguing over who should tell him something that they were obviously both bursting to impart. His progress impeded, Nikolas hoisted them one under each arm and carried them, wriggling and squealing with laughter, up the path to the house.

Just before they arrived there, a young woman emerged, looking slightly flustered and brushing back long black hair from a flushed face. 'Niko! Welcome! Come in, come in.' She lifted her face for the customary kisses, then shook her head in a vaguely apologetic gesture as she smoothed down her dress and led the way into the house. 'I should have been here to stop the boys from swamping you like that. I'm sorry.'

'Oh, please don't be,' Nikolas told her with one of his rare smiles. 'I'm flattered, Sophie; children don't always extend me such an enthusiastic welcome.' For some reason she could not fathom, he glanced at Bethany when he said that, and she found herself hastily avoiding his eyes. Then he turned to Alexia who still, Bethany noticed, looked vaguely uneasy. 'Aunt Alexia, you haven't met Sophie, have you? And these are Heracles' two sons, Dimitri and Pavlos.'

The familiar name brought a responsive tug at Bethany's senses, but almost before she could tell herself that Pavlos was a common enough name in Greece, it was her and Takis's turn to be introduced. Then he caught the young woman's eye and raised an enquiring brow.

The girl nodded. 'He—he's very excited—overcome,' she said in a low and rather breathless voice. 'You understand, Niko?'

Something about this visit disturbed her, but Bethany could not for the moment think what it could be. The children were delightful, and their mother pleasant and rather shy, but whatever the cause, her heart was hammering hard as they entered the house, and there was nothing she could do about the slightly sick feeling she had in her stomach.

The house was as modern inside as out, and it lacked the Oriental air of the old Meandis home, but for all its modernity it suggested comfort and warmth and was very Greek. They were scarcely inside when a man appeared from a room to their left, and at the sight of him Bethany's heart almost stopped beating altogether.

Whether or not Takis had been struck by the same fact, she did not know, for she could not take her eyes off the man as he came across to greet them. In the shadowy coolness of the hall where the light was deceptive, it seemed for a moment that Papa came hurrying towards them, and it was all she could do not to cry out at the feeling it gave her.

A younger, slimmer Papa, it was true, and with a full head of black curly hair instead of the familiar balding tonsure, but with the same warm, welcoming smile showing slightly stained teeth from smoking too many strong cigarettes. It was merely an illusion, of course, and the illusion vanished the moment he got into the better light, but for those few moments the effect had been staggering and quite uncanny.

'Welcome, welcome!' The man drew them into a large airy room whose wide windows opened on to a paved terrace, with a garden beyond. He drew Alexia into a bear-hug and kissed her fondly on both cheeks, then sat her down in an armchair, with almost reverent gentleness. 'It is so good to see you again, my aunt,' he told her, still holding her hands. 'Are you well?'

'I'm well,' Alexia assured him, and studied him with her faded dark eyes for a moment. 'I can see that you thrive, my nephew, and your wife and fine sons too.'

'Yes, yes, yes.' He patted her hands, his head shaking regretfully. 'I wished so much to be there when——' Broad shoulders shrugged helplessly. 'I was in America for business, Aunt Alex, how could I return in the time? But I shall regret it to my dying day.'

'He would have understood; who better?' Alexia assured him softly, and Bethany had no doubt at all that they spoke of her stepfather.

'It is to be hoped,' their host agreed, and turned once more to the rest of his guests. His eyes fell at once on Bethany with her tawny hair and grey eyes, red-gold among the olive darkness of the others. '*Aie!*' he breathed softly, but turned at once, when Nikolas spoke up.

'This is Takis, Heracles.' He drew Takis round in front of him, and just for a second it seemed he hesitated to go on with the introduction. But the man had no such hesitation, he was extending a hand to Takis almost before the introduction was complete. 'Takis,' Nicolas went on, 'this is Heracles Meandis. His mother was your papa's first wife, and he is therefore your half-brother. Do you understand?'

Nikolas seemed to be choosing his words carefully, as well he might, Bethany thought, for her own reaction was one of stunned surprise. Never in all the years she had been close to him and loved him more than she ever had her own father had Pavlos ever mentioned another family. But it was not so much their existence that stunned her but the fact that Papa had managed to keep it so secret. It gave her the curious sensation of having been deceived.

For the moment she was on the edge of events, and

thankfully took time to gather her wits. The situation was between Takis and Heracles Meandis, and even Nikolas it seemed, waited for his reaction with bated breath. Remembering how in times of crisis and doubt they had always turned to Aunt Alexia, Bethany looked for the same reaction from Takis now.

Instead, he twisted his head round and looked up at Nikolas and it was impossible to tell whether the bright gleaming look in his eyes was excitement or a threat of tears. 'I have a brother?' he asked, and Nikolas nodded, his long fingers tensed and curved like claws into the thin boyish shoulders.

'You understand that your papa was married before, many years ago, and had a family.' Nikolas spoke quietly and persuasively, and his tight hold on the boy was reassuring rather than forceful. 'You'll like having grown-up brothers, eh, Takis?'

Nikolas was anxious. Bethany recognised it and it startled her even while she coped with the fact that, in law at least, this man who looked so much like Papa was her brother too. She could recognise too, that Takis was quite ready to accept the sudden change in status, for he was already nodding and starting to smile.

'I think I like it,' he decided. 'I like having a brother, it's something I always wanted!' He turned and beamed his pleasure at Bethany, assuming her to be as happy about it as he was himself, and seeing only the immediate satisfaction of having got the brother he had always wanted. 'We have a brother, Beth, and we didn't know!'

She nodded and smiled, firmly suppressing the feeling that already there was more distance between them than there ever had been before. Nikolas let Takis go and called her forward so that she stood in front of him. 'Bethany is Pavlos's adopted daughter,' he said, and once more Heracles Meandis's dark eyes beamed their appreciation.

'Bethany.' The hands he placed on her shoulders were wide and capable, sculptor's hands like Papa's,

and his smile was as warm as he drew her into his embrace and kissed her cheeks. 'Welcome, sister,' he said,
and looked down at her, smiling widely. 'Welcome,
and be happy!' He studied her for a moment longer,
then shook his head slowly. 'If you look like your
mother, little one, then my father was a very fortunate
man.'

She felt choked by emotion, knowing that for some
reason she had yet to learn, this man had not seen his
father for at least as long as her own knowledge of him.
It was hard to understand why Papa, whom she had
thought she knew so well, had lived apart from his
own child when he had loved children so much.

Stepping back, she was brought up short by Nikolas
standing behind her, and the firm, lean touch of him
was incredibly reassuring she found, even though he
did not put his hands on her, as she wished he would.
His firm strong fingers on her arms would have been
comforting in that moment.

'You find it a little—overwhelming?' Heracles suggested, then laughed and shook his head. 'I too,' he
admitted. 'And it must be quite a shock to suddenly
discover that you have three brothers instead of only
one.'

'Three?'

She looked at him, only vaguely recalling that Nikolas had mentioned brothers, in the plural, only a few
moments ago. 'There were two of us from the first marriage,' Heracles explained. 'My brother Aristides lives
in New York.'

'In America?' Takis pounced on the information
excitedly, and Heracles glanced briefly at Nikolas, as
if seeking his approval before he said anything else.

'For five years now,' he told Takis. 'I have some
photographs for you to see, if you would like that.'

'Oh yes, I would, please!'

He replied without hesitation, and followed Heracles
and his two little sons across the room without a back-
ward glance to include her in the invitation, so that
once again Bethany felt forced outside the familiar,

sharing closeness they had shared. Takis had taken to
his new relations like a duck to water, and it was good
that he had, but it left Bethany with a strange sense of
loss that she could not altogether subdue.

Seeing her family settled, Sophie Meandis murmured something about making coffee, and when she
started for the kitchen Alexia automatically got up
and followed her. When Bethany would have done the
same, however, Nikolas stopped her; a long forefinger
on her arm catching her attention, then pointing to
the open window.

'Come with me into the garden for a few moments,
please,' he said, and she noticed that he kept his voice
fairly low, as if he did not want to distract the small
group gathered in one corner of the room, poring over
a pile of photographs. He must have noticed Alexia's
brief glance over her shoulder as she left the room,
and his last words seemed to be addressed to her as
much as to Bethany. 'It won't take a moment, but I'd
like a few words.'

'Of warning?' Bethany betrayed her uncertainty by
the sharpness of her question, and Nikolas eyed her
steadily.

'As a matter of fact, yes,' he told her quietly. 'I wish
to avoid difficult questions of—time, before it's too
late. Please come with me, Bethany, and try not to look
as if you think I'm about to assault you. You'll give
Heracles quite the wrong impression.'

Bethany walked swiftly across the room with her
back straight and unconsciously stiff, and although
Heracles glanced up briefly as she went out through
the open window and on to the terrace, she noticed
that Takis did not even look up. Nikolas followed,
seemingly casual, with both hands thrust into his
pockets and his dark head tipped slightly upward towards the sun, his eyes half closed.

In such a small garden, it was difficult to find somewhere really private to talk, but the bulk of a flourish-
ing bay tree offered the most likely venue, and the moment they were out of sight of the house, Nikolas came

to a halt. Automatically Bethany turned to face him, though she kept her eyes downcast while he studied her for a moment in silence. When he eventually did speak, it seemed to Bethany that his voice suggested impatience.

'Takis is delighted to discover he has two brothers, as well as nephews,' he said, 'but I gather you're not so pleased, am I right?'

It was a direct challenge and one she was not prepared for, but nevertheless she managed to give him a brief upward glance and shake her head in denial. 'I like Heracles and Sophie, and the two little boys are adorable, but it was rather a—a shock, Nikolas.'

'A shock?' One dark brow condemned her opinion as over-dramatic.

'A surprise, then,' she amended, and showed a hint of impatience herself. 'You must realise that.' Turning her back on him, she walked a few steps until she caught sight of the scene in the living-room when she emerged from the cover of the bay tree. 'If you'd said something about it earlier, even on the way here; you could have, and I'd have been prepared.'

'I intended telling both you and Takis before you met Heracles,' Nikolas told her, 'but when he rang and begged me to bring Takis to meet him this morning, I couldn't very well put him off. He's a good man and a very tolerant one, and he's very genuinely anxious to get to know his young brother. Takis has accepted it very well, so why can't you? I don't begin to understand you, Bethany.'

'You never did, nor ever will!' Bethany declared with a trace of bitterness. Keeping her back to him, she tried in her own way to put her feelings into words, partly because she wanted him to understand, no matter how often she decried the possibility. 'I was so close to Papa for all those years, and he talked to me so often about when he was a boy in Rodos. and what this island was like, compared with Apolidus. I—I would have sworn that he opened his heart to me, more especially when I got older, after my mother left, and yet——' Her voice conveyed exactly her feelings of disillusion, and she turned back to him, but did not yet meet his eyes. 'I realise now that he said very little about his family, but I thought——'

'Did it ever occur to you that he might have a very good reason for not mentioning his family?' Nikolas asked, and she glanced up quickly, sensing something behind the question that made her uneasy.

She had a desperate need to be close to someone, but Nikolas did not reach out and touch her. Physical contact was rare between them, and she had wondered about it at times, for the Greeks were normally such a 'touching' people. Instead he was gazing down at her with a dark, ambiguous look in his eyes.

'Heracles hasn't seen his father since he was thirteen years old, Bethany. It's been that long since Pavlos— made his choice.'

Bethany stared at him, unwilling to believe what he was trying to tell her. Her tongue passed swiftly across her lips and she shook her head in instant denial. 'I don't believe it—not Papa!'

Quietly, Nikolas insisted, 'It's true nevertheless. I'm sorry, Bethany,' he added quickly when he saw the look in her eyes, 'but you're old enough to know the truth, and you're not a stranger to the situation. Your own parents——'

'That's different! Not Papa!'

He let out his breath in a long deep sigh and shook his head. 'You've hidden away on your island too long,' he said quietly. 'You have to get people and situations into the proper perspective or you'll never grow up.'

'If you mean I'll never get hard and cynical like you, I hope I never do!'

On the defensive, she resorted to personal abuse, and the deep gleam in his eyes hardened to determination. 'There is nothing hard and cynical about growing up and facing facts,' he told her. 'And if you're going to understand Takis's situation, you have to know the facts; you have to realise how generous Heracles is being. And he is being so, ironically enough, because he is very like Pavlos, his father.'

'I don't know what you mean.'

'I mean,' Nikolas stressed firmly, 'that Heracles sees the rights as well as the wrongs of the situation, and acts accordingly. You see the world and the people around you through rose-coloured spectacles. Except possibly in my own case,' he added with a touch of sardonic humour. 'It's time you came down to earth, Bethany.'

'There's nothing wrong with the way I live.' Her voice quivered uncertainly, and she wished there was somewhere she could turn to get away from him. 'I know you don't agree with the way Papa brought me up, but he was kind and understanding, and I loved him.'

'Of course you did,' Nikolas agreed, 'and he was all you say he was. But he wasn't the saint you insist on making him out to be, Bethany, and he would have been the last person to want such a reputation. Pavlos was a lusty, vital man who lived life as *he* wanted to, regardless of convention or family, or anything else.'

'*No!*' She yelled her defiance at him because she could not face what he was trying to make her see, and he took both her hands in his when she clasped them together, drawing her towards him.

'Bethany!' He resisted her struggles, his strong fingers gripping her hard, and when she looked up she saw the firm set of his mouth, but shook her head in disbelief over the unexpected pity she saw mingled with determination in his eyes. She refused to accept anything that undermined her blind adoration of her stepfather, but Nikolas was all too convincing. 'Listen to me!' He held her tightly, fighting to hold her attention. 'Pavlos loved you, he had a great capacity for love and you were a child in need of loving. He was a kindly, gentle man, but he was a man, Bethany, not a god! Don't you understand that? He was everything you thought him, except perfect—no man is that!

That's why he didn't mention his first family to you,
because you adored him and he was afraid you'd think
less of him–if you knew.'

There was a dark, wary look in her eyes that mis-
trusted him still, even while her common sense recognised that what he said was true. She looked up at him
and shook her head. 'You're so—so implacable,' she
whispered accusingly. 'You scarcely knew Papa.'

'But I *knew* him, Bethany, that's my whole point.'

She was shaking her head slowly, her hands still im-
prisoned by his strong fingers, and strangely enough
there was a kind of comfort in the contact. 'You didn't
approve of the way he brought us up,' she said in a
light, almost childlike voice, 'but you can't know how
perfect it was there with just the four of us. With Papa
gone, Aunt Alex and I could have cared for Takis until he becomes a man. We could have gone on as we
were, we don't need you!'

'*You* could have gone on hiding from the rest of the
world,' Nikolas told her, tight-lipped, 'but what of
Takis? Doesn't he deserve more?'

'He was happy!' She was fighting a losing battle and
she knew it, but she had to go on.

'*You* were happy in your way,' Nikolas corrected her
relentlessly. 'I doubt if you even stopped to think
whether Takis was. I hadn't realised until now, just
how fearful you are of the outside world or of any kind
of change. I'm not belittling Pavlos or your precious
little island, Bethany, I'm simply trying to make you
see beyond your very limited horizon; to try and bring
you into the same world the rest of us live in.'

Her hands were still held firmly clasped between his,
as if he feared she might try to escape if he let her go,
and she looked up at him with shimmering grey eyes.
'Is that why you brought me out here?' she whispered.
'To—bring me down to earth? Oh, you're cruel, Nikolas! You're even more cruel than I realised!'

He apparently ignored the charge of cruelty, although his mouth tightened a little more, and fixed
her with a steady, implacable gaze. 'I wanted you to

be fully informed before I make my plans known to Takis,' he told her. 'You're older and, I'd hoped, just as intelligent. I hope he won't try to work things out for himself yet, and I didn't want you to mention things like Pavlos being married three times, or when and where. I know women have a mania for details like that.'

She wasn't thinking as clearly as usual, and Bethany frowned at him in confusion. 'I don't understand.'

Nikolas glanced, almost involuntarily, she suspected, at the group in the living-room, still absorbed with looking at photographs. 'You can see how much Takis likes company,' he said, 'just as Pavlos did, and he needs more than Apolidus can offer in the way of education. I intend to send him to school here and, it is to be hoped, on to university.'

'You're going to send him away?'

'Do you imagine he's going to weep like a woman about it?' Nikolas demanded, harshly impatient. He must have noticed the look in her eyes then, for he reached out suddenly and stroked his long fingers down her soft cheek. 'He'll enjoy it, Bethany, and you know it, don't you?'

There was no way she could deny it, for Takis had enjoyed the occasions when neighbours or friends from the artists' colony called to see them and the talking and drinking went on far into the night. He was, as Nikolas said, like Papa in that respect, but it seemed everything was being turned upside down suddenly, and she found it hard to cope with the changes.

'If you say so,' she shrugged obligingly, then remembered something he had said when they first came out there. 'I suppose the—delicate matter you wanted to talk about was that Papa left home?' she said, and Nikolas nodded, just for the moment avoiding her eyes.

'Not only that,' he said. 'It's what I meant about not talking about weddings and dates. Neither Sophie nor Aunt Alexia will, they know better, but you might inadvertently make things awkward by being curious.

Pavlos was a widower when he married your mother, you knew that?'

She nodded. 'Takis's mother had died when he was born; she'd been dead about a year when Papa re-married.'

The hands holding hers squeezed more tightly for a moment. 'Pavlos had been widowed only about three months when he married your mother, Bethany. That was when his wife, Heracles' mother, died.'

It took a second or two for it to dawn on her, but when it did Bethany's eyes darted quickly to where Takis sat, lovingly surrounded by his new family. 'Oh no!' she whispered.

'He mustn't know, Bethany, not yet.' Nikolas's quiet voice broke in to her stunned mind. 'But he can't remain hidden away on Apolidus for the rest of his life, he's entitled to the same advantages his brothers had. Heracles is anxious to take him into his home while he's over here at school, and I think—I know he'll be happy. It's what Pavlos really wanted for him.'

She nodded, too overcome for words suddenly, for everything seemed to be disintegrating around her since Papa's death, and she longed to flee back home before every shred of her familiar world disappeared. She felt as she had so often done as a very small child, that there was no real place for her, no familiar place or faces that made her feel secure. The tip of her tongue flicked anxiously across her lips again, and she looked up at Nikolas with eyes that had a curiously lost look.

'And me?' she ventured in a barely audible whisper. 'What about me, Nikolas?'

For a moment it seemed, he wavered, although it was unlike him to do anything so negative, then he looked steadily into her eyes. 'What do you want to do?' he asked, and the question seemed so much like a lifeline that she answered it unhesitatingly.

'I'd like to go home,' she said.

# CHAPTER FOUR

BETHANY did her best not to let anyone else but Nikolas see how much she was affected by the rapidly changing circumstances since her stepfather's death, and she
convinced herself that she succeeded. Her rather plain-
tive request to be allowed to go home to Apolidus had
been neither refused out of hand nor yet complied
with. But common sense suggested that whatever Nikolas's final decision concerning her future, they must go
back to the island, at least for a while until everything
was settled, and she pinned all her hopes on that.

Takis was wildly excited about the whole prospect.
His horizon had suddenly broadened beyond his
wildest dreams, and he could hardly be blamed for
making the most of it. He seemed not to notice that
Bethany was less responsive than usual to his enthusi-
asm, probably because they were now much less de-
pendent upon one another for company, and less close.

With Takis involved in his own plans, Theo sought
to monopolise Bethany, and it was he who suggested
that they go for a drive somewhere, a few mornings
later. He looked frankly taken aback, however, when
she took his question of where they should go seriously, and named Kamiros; evidently he had expected
to have the choice left to him.

She had a naïveté that was as strange to him as his
sophistication was to her, and when consulted, she had
gone rapidly through the names of places she knew in
Rhodes, and come up with Kamiros. Her stepfather
had spoken of the ancient city and she knew it was
only a short drive to get there, so she had not stopped
to consider any possible objection to her choice.

'Ruins?' said Theo, making his opinion of the venue
quite clear, so that she felt strangely gauche suddenly.

'Papa told me about it,' Bethany told him, 'and I've

73

always wanted to see it.' She eyed him uncertainly, not understanding his frown. 'That is—if you don't mind, Theo.'

He shrugged, but although he yielded it was pretty plain that he had misgivings. 'As long as you come with me I don't really mind where we go,' he said, making the best of a bad job.

But his plans were to receive a further setback when they joined the rest of the family for breakfast and Nikolas learned of the proposed trip. 'You'll be taking Takis with you, of course?' He made it an indisputable fact, not a question, and Bethany had no doubt at all that what he really meant was that she and Theo were not to be allowed to go for their drive alone. 'Aunt Alexia can't go with you, I know,' Nikolas went on, 'I'm driving her to see an old friend, and Aunt Helen and Uncle Gregori have other plans, so it will have to be Takis.'

'I don't see why it has to be anybody,' Bethany objected, glaring at him in annoyance. 'I surely don't need a chaperone to go and look at ruins, Nikolas. Surely I'm to be trusted that far—I'm not a baby!'

She heard Aunt Alexia's faintly indrawn breath, and felt a twinge of irritation, but Nikolas was as adamant as she expected him to be. 'If you were,' he answered coolly, 'I would be less concerned. But as you say, you are *not* a baby, and Theo has a certain— reputation among pretty young women. That their families have little care for their reputations is their concern, but you are my concern, and you'll counter any chance of gossip by taking Takis with you.'

Aunt Alexia, she could guess, was in accord with his decision, but it was much more difficult to tell where Nurmina Meandis's sympathies lay, and the other aunt and her husband would not dream of expressing an opinion. Bethany did not altogether understand her own reaction either. She resented his interference, his curb on her freedom of choice, and yet at the same time it gave her a curious feeling of satisfaction that she made no attempt to fathom at the moment.

Briefly he glanced up from his breakfast and caught her eye. 'We've been through all this before, Bethany,' he reminded her.

He had not once raised his voice, and yet there was no disputing the finality of his decision; even so Bethany found it irresistible to have one last try. 'We're going to Kamiros,' she told him. 'Papa told me it always attracts tourists, so there are bound to be other people about.'

He caught and held her gaze again for a moment, adamant and unyielding. 'Nevertheless Takis will come with you,' he insisted quietly. 'I remember you told me that the two of you had unearthed some kind of temple in Apolidus, so you're both interested in archaeology; isn't that right, Takis?' Takis nodded, although quite clearly he was far from happy at the prospect of playing chaperon. 'Good! Then I'm sure you'll enjoy it.'

'Being chaperoned around a lot of ruins wasn't what I had in mind,' Theo grumbled, and just for a moment a gleam of amusement showed in Nikolas's dark eyes when he looked across at him.

'I'm quite sure it isn't what you had in mind,' he told him smoothly. 'It's because I know exactly what you *did* have in mind that Takis is coming with you. And as Bethany chose Kamiros, it's obvious she wishes to go there, so I'm sure you won't want to change your plans and disappoint her, Theo.'

Seeing himself defeated, Theo murmured his excuses, but as he got up from the table he gave his brother a bright and frankly malicious smile. 'Are you so sure I *would* have disappointed her?' he asked, and glancing quickly across at Nikolas, Bethany saw his lips tighten for a moment before he replied.

'Possibly not,' he allowed coolly, 'but I hold less liberal views than yours. Theo, and I happen to be Bethany's guardian; which is perhaps fortunate for her!'

Theo paused briefly, glaring in frustration at the dark head that was again bent over while Nikolas gave his attention to his breakfast once more. Theo glanced at his mother, seeking her support, Bethany guessed, but Nurmina Meandis kept heavy lids lowered and did not see the appeal, perhaps deliberately.

Defeated, Theo shrugged in irritation and turned to go. 'I'd better go and change into more suitable shoes if I'm to go trekking over stony terrain with a chaperon in tow.' He strode off across the patio, turning after a moment to look back at his brother's dark, resolute face, made even less encouraging by the shadow of the trees that clustered about the wide patio. 'Is it allowed that we take a picnic lunch?' he asked, and although Nikolas looked up at once, Bethany noticed that he hesitated briefly before he answered.

'Of course,' he said.

Nurmina Meandis had said nothing during the exchange, and yet she was not a woman to be easily subdued if she had something to say, Bethany guessed, so presumably she had seen nothing amiss in her son's behaviour. Instead her dusky, rather severe features wore a faint smile, almost as if it amused her. She doted on her younger son, that much was evident in her treatment of him, but there was a lot of difference in age between him and Nikolas, and apparently Nikolas had taken on the role normally undertaken by the father. Judging by that smile, Nurmina was content for him to do so.

They took a picnic lunch with them, as Theo had suggested, and the basket was packed with bread, cheese and salad, a cold chicken and some luscious home-grown cherries for dessert, as well as a bottle of retsina. By the time they set out Bethany was beginning to feel the fluttering thrill of anticipation, and Theo's surreptitious wink as they walked out to the car suggested that he had recovered his good humour and was prepared to make the best of it, chaperon or not.

Takis obviously did not care for the position of unwelcome third party, but he had learned by now not to argue with his implacable guardian, and when Theo dumped the picnic basket on to the back seat of the car beside him, he nudged Takis in the ribs and winked an eye. 'Take heart, cousin!' he told him cheerfully, then slid into the driver's seat and smiled at Bethany as he started the engine. 'We have a call to make on our way, but it shouldn't take very long—a few seconds only.'

To Bethany the route they took seemed familiar, and when they eventually drew up in front of a bright new white house, she realised that the call they had to make was at Heracles' home. Theo got out, murmuring an apology before he left them, then reappeared a few moments later beaming and very obviously pleased with himself. Opening the rear door of the car, he peered in at Takis.

'I've seen Sophie,' he told him. 'She says Heracles is taking the boys to see football when he comes back— wouldn't you rather watch football than go to Kamiros, Takis?'

Bethany turned swiftly in her seat and caught Takis's faintly rebellious eye. 'Takis!' He shrugged, and she appealed to Theo, though not very hopefully. 'Theo, we can't, not when——'

'Bah!' He waved her to silence with a careless hand, laughing as he stepped aside to let Takis out of the car. 'Every man to his own pleasures, cousin! I know Heracles will be delighted to take him to see football, and I don't have to ask which Takis would rather do.'

'Football!' Takis declared unhesitatingly, but Bethany noticed that he carefully avoided her eye as he got out of the car.

He knew as well as any of them why Nikolas had sent him as chaperon, but at the moment, apparently, he was prepared to take the risk of angering him so that he could go to football with Heracles. In her heart Bethany couldn't blame him, but she knew how angry Nikolas would be if he ever learned of the deception, and she had the uneasy feeling that it was all too possible he would find out. He had a discomfiting knack of discovering facts he wasn't intended to.

'Nikolas is going to be furious, Theo.' She put her doubts into words as he got back into the car, but Theo laughed, waving a hand to Takis as he restarted the engine.

'Only if he finds out,' he told her, and turned a beamingly confident smile in her direction. 'Be happy, cousin! We have the whole day to ourselves, and we'll collect Takis on our way back. No one will be any wiser.'

Far from reassured, Bethany sat back. She was not so naïve as to suppose Theo had rid himself of Takis's company simply because he resented taking along a chaperon, and she felt vaguely uneasy that he had gone to such trouble. She had had very little experience of men in the romantic sense, but there was little doubt what was in Theo's mind; his satisfied smile spoke for itself, and the gleaming darkness of his eyes sent curious little shivers of anticipation running through her as they took the coast road to Kamiros.

To reach the ruined city itself, however, it was necessary to climb on foot, and as they walked up the sloping path Theo once more raised his voice in complaint. 'There are so many more comfortable ways of spending a day,' he grumbled as he coped with the picnic basket as well as the incline, but Bethany turned a flushed face and smiled at him.

'I've always wanted to come here,' she told him, 'and you can't possibly be tired yet, Theo.'

He made no answer, but they left the basket presently, and climbed on to look down at the ruined city of Kamiros, sprawled downwards towards the sea between high ridges of pine trees. It was incredible to Bethany that they could stand and look down at a city that had stood there two thousand years before and still see the actual streets and houses, each facing into its own courtyard.

A market, and temples to the various gods, all clearly defined, even though the walls for the most part were little more than a couple of feet high. The main street of wide shallow steps went upward towards a ruined temple, now little more than six slender columns fused in golden stone against a fierce blue sky, and linked by a narrow ledge of roof.

It was peaceful too, and she closed her eyes for a moment to absorb the soft moan of the wind in the pine trees and the clear piping song of the birds. Crickets trilled somewhere among the sparse, sunscorched grass, and in the background was the murmur of water running through the underground pipes and cisterns of the ancient plumbing system. The faint mumble of other human voices was too distant to be disturbing and she felt delightfully relaxed and lazy.

She was glad she had persuaded Theo to bring her, and she was smiling to herself as she opened her eyes and gazed once more at the six pillars that crowned the summit of the hill. Someone stood among them, barely discernible; a man, tall and curiously familiar, and she recalled with a start having seen him before. She remembered quite clearly, on the harbour when they arrived, the man who had seemed to be watching her, and she made a small involuntary sound, because he still looked vaguely familiar and she still could not think why he should.

Theo turned quickly when he heard her indrawn breath. But he looked at her rather than following the direction of her gaze, and in the time that elapsed between her recognition and his response, the man vanished, leaving Bethany gazing at a skyline bereft of human form. It was curious how familiar the man had seemed that first time and now again, and yet she was willing to swear she had never seen him before that time on the harbour wall.

'Bethany?' Theo squeezed her hand with his slim cool fingers and she turned quickly and smiled at him. 'What's the matter?'

'Nothing's the matter.'

She glanced just briefly once more at the top of the hill, then shook her head, convinced she had imagined the coincidence. Or perhaps the man was a member of the artist colony at home, that would account for his

being familiar. Whatever the reason, it wasn't important, and they did not have the ancient city to themselves, despite its peace and quiet; the man could have
been anybody.

As she turned away the picture of the man on the
hilltop was already fading in her mind, but Theo still
looked at her curiously, and she hastened to explain.
'I noticed someone standing up there on the top of the
hill for a moment, that's all.'

'Someone you know?'

She shook her head, though she was not certain,
even now. 'No, but he startled me for a moment, that's
all.'

'Oh, I see!' Theo laughed and put a hand beneath
her arm, drawing her off, down the steps to where they
had left their picnic. 'You're imagining visitations
from the ancient gods! Well, watch out, my lovely
cousin, you know what *they* were like with beautiful
women!' The hand under her arm slid down and en-
folded her fingers in a firm clasp, and his dark eyes
beamed warmly down at her, bringing more immediate possibilities to mind. 'If you had let me take you
to a quiet little beach somewhere, where we could
have been quite alone instead of constantly in danger
of being discovered by tourists, you would not have
had to dream of being ravished by the gods!'

Bethany hoped she didn't blush too obviously, for
she felt Theo would find it an amusing novelty, and
she didn't want to appear too naïve. 'I'm perfectly
happy with my present situation, thank you,' she told
him, smiling at his reproachfully pouting lower lip
and small frown. 'It's everything Papa said it was, and
I'm glad I came. And I can't imagine a more romantic
place for our picnic, can you?'

'Quite easily!' Theo glared at a couple who were
walking along the width of the steps, and for a moment his likeness to Nikolas when he frowned so disapprovingly like that, was vaguely discomfiting. He sat
down and leaned his back against sun-warmed stones,
obviously determined to complain. 'This is a favourite

place of tourists, Bethany; we shall have people on top of us all the time.'

'Well, I like it!' She set about unpacking their picnic, a task that Theo made no effort to assist in, and as she handed him his meal and a glass of wine, she glanced at him surreptitiously. For all his professed liberalism, Theo Meandis was traditional enough when it suited him. He looked up and caught her eye, and she smiled. 'I'm grateful to you for bringing me here, Theo, really.'

He sat down with one knee drawn up and supporting an elbow, holding a chicken leg in his two hands for a moment while he regarded her steadily. 'How grateful, Bethany?' he asked softly, and she leaned swiftly to delve again into the basket rather than let him see her flushed cheeks.

'Shall we eat?' she suggested, and Theo laughed.

Lunch did a great deal to restore Theo's good humour, and he leaned back against the wall of a two-thousand-year-old villa wearing the satisfied smile of the replete. His eyelids drooped lazily as he watched Bethany pack up the picnic basket, and his mouth curved into a languid and frankly sensual smile.

'You're beautiful, cousin,' he murmured, and reached out for a strand of her hair, letting it run through his fingers. 'Was your mama as beautiful as you? Is that why Pavlos married again, because she was irresistible?'

In view of what Nikolas had told her about her stepfather's matrimonial tangles, it wasn't a subject that Bethany wanted to discuss, and she shook her head. 'I couldn't say. Who knows why anyone marries anyone else?'

'Very profound,' Theo teased, still smiling lazily, and again ran a strand of her hair through his fingers. '*Was* she as beautiful as you, Bethany?'

Bethany tossed back her hair out of his reach and closed the lid of the basket. Her heart was drumming

wildly and she did not stop to choose her words. 'Nikolas says not!'

Theo widened his eyes for a moment and regarded
her in silence. 'Does he?' he drawled. 'And did he
know your mama too?'

Still on her knees, Bethany turned to put the basket
to one side, finding the subject oddly disturbing. 'No,'
she said, 'but he *has* seen the portrait my father—my
real father, painted of her. It's a very good likeness, as
I remember her.'

'You're something of a mystery woman, aren't you?'
he asked, and Bethany looked up, meeting the dark
and faintly mocking eyes for a moment. 'The girl from
nowhere.'

Bethany got to her feet. She was wary of that hint of
mockery and unwilling as always to talk about any
part of her existence before the settled life she had
known with her stepfather. Indeed she neither knew
nor cared to try and remember very much about her
previous existence, but nor was she happy about ad-
mitting it in the circumstances.

'I don't know that I'm such a mystery,' she told him,
brushing down her dress and trying to sound cool and
matter-of-fact. 'I'm English, or at least Welsh. My
mother's name was Megan, and that's a Welsh name, I
know.'

'And your father?' Theo probed softly.

She tossed back her hair and there was a firm look
about her mouth as she looked up at the columns of
the ruined temple on the skyline, determined to
change the subject. 'I don't remember him,' she said,
and hurried on before he could comment. 'I'd like to
walk to the very top of the hill, Theo. Are you coming?'

'No.'

He sat with his head leaned back and regarded her
below heavy lids, making it clear that he expected her
to be guided by his feelings. As if to test her reaction
he stretched out a hand to her, and smiled lazily, his

long fingers curled persuasively, his shadowed dark eyes seductively inviting.

'Come and sit by me, Bethany.'

He looked so confident, so sure that she was going to give in, but something in his smile sent a trickling shiver along her spine, and she shook her head instinctively. She dodged the hand that reached to take her wrist and walked a step or two past him, turning to speak over her shoulder.

'Laze if you want to,' she told him in a slightly breathless voice, 'I'm going to the top of the hill.'

'Bethany!'

In other circumstances she might have found his reaction laughable, just as she did the boldly admiring calls and whistles of the fishermen on the quay at home. Theo looked not only surprised but petulant, and there was nothing she could do about the little smile that touched the corners of her mouth as she started to mount the wide shallow steps of the old city's main street.

Whether or not he changed his mind and followed, she did not bother to find out, but climbed right to the summit and stood looking down at the changing colours of the Aegean as it spread out from the shore. A dazzling peacock blue close inshore, and rich deep amethyst further out; a rich, beautiful ocean that seemed always to have been part of her life.

Maybe it was the effect of more retsina than she was accustomed to, as well as the breathtaking scenery, that made her feel slightly heady, but the instant she caught the sound of footsteps behind her, she thought of the man she had seen standing up there earlier and swung round quickly. Too quickly, as it happened, for she lost her footing and before she could save herself she went tumbling down the slope until she was brought up sharply and painfully by the stump of a fluted pillar some three or four metres below, and the breath knocked out of her.

'Bethany!' Only when she heard Theo cry out did she realise whose footsteps she had heard on the steps

behind her, and she lay there for a moment too dazed
to move and conscious of a dull pain in her left side.
Theo came swiftly down the ancient steps in a sideways gait to balance himself, then dropped on to one
knee and bent over her anxiously. 'Bethany, are you
hurt?'

Too winded to answer him for the moment, she
shook her head, not even attempting to get up off the
ground, and as she moved her head she caught sight
of someone else coming quickly down the steps, with
that same curious sideways gait. 'Niko!' she whispered,
not even sure if he heard her, but Theo turned his
head quickly.

'Holy Mother!' He murmured the prayer as he
stood upright, and Nikolas came hurrying down to
join them, dropping on to one knee beside her, just
as Theo had.

'What happened?' he demanded, barking the question at his brother while he gave his attention to Bethany.

'She fell from the top,' Theo explained, and already
his voice had a suggestion of defensiveness, as if he
realised he would be called to account for the accident.
'Something startled her—someone; I don't know.'

Nikolas glared back over his shoulder. 'You
didn't——'

'No, damn it, I didn't!' Theo declared angrily, but
Nikolas offered no apology.

As he turned back to Bethany, his expression was
more fiercely angry than she had ever seen it. He was
breathing hard too, as he crouched beside her, and she
noticed that the speed of his descent had dislodged a
thick swathe of black hair, so that it swept down over
one eye and covered half his brow.

'You could have broken your neck!' he breathed, as
if the possibility only now occurred to him.

In other circumstances Bethany thought she might
have suggested the remark was wishful thinking, but
she was still feeling dazed and her left side still hurt,
though it was easing just a little, she thought. Instead

she made an attempt to sit up, and caught her breath sharply when he pressed his hands to her shoulders and forced her back on to the ground.

'Stay where you are for a moment,' he insisted, 'until I see what damage has been done. Do you hurt anywhere?'

Bethany ignored her aching side and shook her head automatically. Not that she really expected him to take her word for it, and she made only a barely audible murmur when he pressed on. Monosyllabic questions and answers determined that her legs and arms were unhurt apart from a graze or two, but when he placed his hands on her ribs, she cried involuntarily.

'That hurts?' Long fingers probed carefully, and Bethany gnawed at her lower lip but said nothing, only nodded her head. 'Is it bad?'

She swallowed hard, hastening to deny it. 'It's better than it was, Nikolas, honestly. I'm not hurt—not seriously.'

Seemingly she wasn't believed, for the gentle probing continued for another second or two before he pronounced himself satisfied. 'Can you breathe without pain?' he asked, and she nodded her head again, summoning a faint smile from somewhere.

'Are you a doctor as well as a lawyer?' she asked, and realised how small and breathless her voice sounded.

Ignoring her question, Nikolas put his hands behind her and raised her into a sitting position, watching her face as he did so for signs of hurt. Bethany felt better sitting up, but she was alarmingly conscious of the muscular arm that supported her and the warmth of the body she rested against. Reaching down with his free hand he once more laid his long fingers over the area below the curve of her breast, his palm warm and firm through the thin dress she wore.

'I think you've escaped with nothing worse than bruising.' he told her. 'You've been very lucky to escape so lightly.'

There was a rapid and unfamiliar urgency to her heartbeat, Bethany realised, and glanced up at the dark face close to her own, catching an expression in his eyes that was even more disturbing. 'Can I—can I stand up now?' she asked in a soft small voice, and he nodded.

The supporting arm slid a little further round her and he used his other hand to assist him in raising her to her feet, still supporting her when she stood. Her legs felt shaky and she clung to him unhesitatingly, Theo's presence in the background completely forgotten for a moment while she sought to recover her composure. So far his anger was confined to the gleaming darkness of his eyes, but she could guess that once he was certain of her recovery he would give vent to it.

He had said nothing yet about Takis, but it would come very soon now, she knew, and with the idea of delaying the moment as long as possible, she prolonged her recovery. Resting her head on his chest, she turned her face to the smooth softness of his shirt. His dash down the steps, his anger and also his anxiety all contributed to a burning heat that emanated from him, and her cheek throbbed with the hard, steady beat of his heart as he held her close for a moment.

'Can you stand alone?'

There was a throaty harshness in his voice that she took to be yet another sign of his anger, and she nodded, though she was reluctant to move away. 'Yes, I think so.' She experimented, found she was much more steady than she realised, and nodded. 'I'm all right, Nikolas.'

As if her recovery was a sign for him to bring matters to a head, Theo spoke up quickly, his voice harsh and resentful. 'How long have you been around?' he asked, Nikolas. 'Were you Bethany's mystery man? The one she saw at the top of the hill earlier?'

'No, of course it wasn't Nikolas!' Bethany stepped in quickly, and answered Nikolas's frown with a hasty explanation. 'I noticed someone up here just before we had lunch, and I thought I recognised him—I thought it might have been the same man I saw on the harbour when we arrived.'

'And was it?'

She shook her head. 'No. I mean, I don't know really. He just looked vaguely familiar somehow, like he did last time I saw him, but I don't know him, I'm sure I don't.' She laughed uneasily, wanting the subject dropped even if it meant bringing Nikolas's anger down on them both. 'When I heard someone behind me just now I wondered——' She lifted her shoulders uneasily. 'It must have been Theo—I didn't know he'd followed me; I turned too quickly and missed my footing.'

Nikolas frowned curiously at his brother, then at her. 'Wasn't Theo with you?'

'No.' She too glanced at Theo and deliberately avoided telling Nikolas that she had left his brother sulking because she wouldn't stay and let herself succumb to that undoubted charm of his. 'I wanted to walk to the top of the hill, and Theo didn't, so—I came on my own. I might have known he'd follow me.'

'You might have known,' Nikolas echoed. 'And you knew it wouldn't be Takis, of course.'

His voice sent little trills of ice-water trickling along her spine, and it was all too easy to realise that he knew exactly where Takis was and why he had been left behind. It was instinctive when she lifted her chin the way she did and looked at him with a sparkling glint of defiance in her eyes.

'You know he isn't here, Nikolas, or *you* wouldn't be here!'

'Don't be clever, Bethany—not with me!' Although he still held his anger firmly in check, it burned fiercely behind his eyes. But it was not from fear of him that she trembled, it was from some strange reaction she did not even pretend to understand. 'I called in to see Heracles, and Sophie told me he'd taken the boys to see a football match.' His eyes narrowed and they concentrated on her so unwaveringly that Bethany hastily looked away. 'Unfortunately for you, Sophie isn't as glibly deceitful as you probably hoped, and she let slip that Takis had gone with them. Or I should say fortunately for you.'

'So you came chasing after us, fearing the worst!'

Theo issued the challenge rashly, and Nikolas half turned his head, his opinion unmistakable.

'As you would expect,' he said, his cool control contrasting sharply with Theo's obvious discomfiture. 'Oh, I don't have to be told whose idea it was to leave Takis behind with Heracles, I'm fully aware of how devious you can be, brother, but I've no doubt Bethany fell in with your plans willingly enough. Didn't you, Bethany?'

'No, she didn't, as it happens!' Theo denied firmly. 'If you must know Bethany tried to dissuade me from leaving Takis behind because she said you'd be furious!' His eyes gleamed maliciously as he watched his brother's sternly set features. 'She seems to be afraid of you for some reason—a reason that no doubt you understand better than I do!'

Bethany was shaking like a leaf, but it was not from fear, as Theo suggested, although being fixed with those fierce dark eyes did nothing to help her composure. 'You don't have to defend me, Theo,' she told him, 'Nikolas is always ready to believe the worst of me. Nevertheless, I still deny he has the right to——'

'I have every right to be angry when arrangements made for your protection are deliberately flouted,' Nikolas told her harshly.

'I don't *need* to be protected, Nikolas, I've told you that!'

His head shook slowly. 'Too much freedom, too little guidance, and no experience of men—— Bah! I have need to be angry! And you, brother.' He turned on Theo and his lip curled angrily. 'Just two days and you are finding ways to seduce your cousin!'

'Oh no, Niko!' Bethany reached instinctively and put a hand on his arm to draw his attention back to her. But when she saw the look in his eyes, she drew back hastily. 'Theo brought me to see the old city because I wanted to see it, that's all.'

Nikolas gazed at her in silence for a moment, then he shook his head slowly. 'Holy Mother!' he breathed piously. 'Can you really be such a child?'

Bethany's gaze darted beyond him to Theo, and she knew that Nikolas was right; Theo had had seduction in mind, and she had known it when she came with him. The reason she had not protested more vigorously when he left Takis at Heracles's, was because she had been reluctant to let Theo see her as too inexperienced and naïve to go with him alone.

'I'm old enough to look after myself,' she said in a small voice, then winced at Nikolas's sharp bark of laughter.

'Fortunately for you, I don't agree,' he told her harshly. 'And if you've seen all you wish to see here, I'll drive you back.' It was automatic to glance at Theo, and Nikolas caught the look. 'Theo has to collect Takis when he returns from the football match,' he said, and glanced at his wristwatch. 'If you start now, Theo, you should be in time to meet them as they come out.'

Theo's handsome features were distorted for a moment in a furious scowl, and he glared at his brother with narrowed eyes. 'I don't see the difference,' he stated clearly and firmly, 'in Bethany being alone with you or with me. If you——'

'I'm exercising the privilege of a guardian,' Nikolas told him, 'and Bethany has no need to fear any action of mine.'

'I see!' Theo's eyes gleamed maliciously. 'And does Bethany know that you're not quite the paragon of virtue you seem? Does she know of *your* predilection for beautiful women, or have you omitted to mention that point? Of course,' Theo went on, his thirst for vengeance making him rash, 'you prefer something a little more—sophisticated as a rule, don't you? So maybe she's safe with you after all!'

Bethany could feel her heart thudding at her ribs as if it would burst free, and the throbbing ache in her left side caught at her breath so that she put a hand to it as she stared aghast at Theo's flushed and angry face. Nikolas's staggering self-control had never been more sorely tried, but still he managed to remain calm, cool even, although his eyes blazed with a fury that made her tremble.

'If you leave right away,' he told Theo in a flat, cold voice, 'you should still catch them on the way out.'

Theo hesitated, glanced at Bethany as if he expected her support, then shrugged and turned away. Striding down the slope where the car was parked and leaving her there with Nikolas. There was a burning fury in Nikolas that was almost tangible, and she said nothing to bring his attention back to her, only stood and waited to see what he would do.

He watched Theo's angrily striding figure until he disappeared lower down the hill, then turned swiftly and caught her looking at him. The colour flooded into her face and she hastily looked away, but she was unprepared for the hand that slid beneath her chin suddenly and raised her face to searching dark eyes.

'You're shocked?' he asked, and a hint of gentleness in his voice both startled and touched her. 'By what Theo said about me?'

She wanted to ease away from the firm fingers, but it wasn't as easy as she hoped. Keeping her eyes downcast, she answered him truthfully. 'I suppose I am, in a way ,' she confessed, and heard him expel his breath in a sigh of resignation. 'And yet I suppose I shouldn't be,' she added hastily, before he decided that his own belief in her innocence had been confirmed. 'You are a man, after all.'

There was no one else about, only the cool wind in the trees and the persistent chirping of the crickets in the warm grass, and Nikolas laid his long fingers against her cheek lightly, stroking downward until small shivers ran through her body and she clenched her hands tightly. 'I'm a man,' he agreed softly, and just for a moment a gleam of white teeth teased her for her simplicity. 'And because I am, I'm going to drive you home, just as I told Theo I would. Because I'm not going to give him or anyone else the slightest reason to doubt my suitability as your guardian. Come!'

'Nikolas——'

'No arguments, please, Bethany!' He took her arm to help her on the steps, his grip reminding her that she had sustained quite a few bruises during her fall. 'Can you manage the climb down?'

Her face flushed, and feeling resentful of his determination to play the stern guardian, Bethany looked up at him with a glint of challenge in her eyes. 'Suppose I can't?' she asked.

He said nothing, only came to a halt suddenly and turned to face her on the worn stone steps, regarding her for a moment in a way that made her shake her head slowly from side to side without having the least idea why she did it. Then he bent suddenly and lifted her off her feet and into his arms, his hard fingers pressing into the tender spot over her ribs so that she caught her breath.

'Niko!'

She clung to him tightly, one arm about his neck as he made his way down the rest of the incline, her heart thudding wildly as she nestled against firm, warm flesh through a thin shirt. His car was parked close by where Theo's had been, and he stood her on her feet while he opened the door, sliding his hand from her waist in a stroking movement that skimmed the curve of her breast.

The door open, he held it for her, dark eyes watching with gleaming intensity as she stood there, too dazed for the moment to move. 'Get in!' he told her, and slammed the door closed the moment she swung her legs inside. 'And don't ever play those games with Theo, or I will personally see that you get the beating of your life! Do you hear me girl?'

'I hear you!' Bethany waited until he came round and slid into the seat beside her, uncertain what the emotions were that churned chaotically inside her. She glanced at the dark, slightly Oriental profile and tried to still the sudden almost choking urgency of her heart. As he started the car's engine, she found her voice and her courage and challenged his warning in a small, uncertain voice. 'What I don't understand is why you condemn Theo for behaving as you do.'

With the engine just ticking over, Nikolas turned and looked at her silently for a moment, then he shook his head. Again giving the impression that he found her naïveté hard to believe, 'Not as I do,' he said quietly but firmly. 'Theo would not have resisted the temptation you offered back there, Bethany, that is the difference.' She began to protest that she had not intended any such thing, but then realised just how intentional her provocation had been, and hastily lowered her eyes to the hands on her lap. 'I'm glad you're beginning to realise your own potency,' Nikolas told her. 'But have a care how you use it, little one.' He reached over and squeezed her hand, his strong fingers again arousing that alarming flutter of excitement in her. 'I'll take you home,' he said, and Bethany wished he meant it.

She suddenly felt very vulnerable and, as she always did at such times, she thought of Apolidus as her haven, even if Papa wasn't there any more. Nikolas did not inspire the same kind of feeling at all.

# CHAPTER FIVE

APOLIDUS looked so very tiny at a distance, but from the moment it first appeared as a green dot on the ocean Bethany never took her eyes off it. In a surprisingly short time the summit of its dominating hill loomed hazily against the sky, then white mushroom dots became recognisable as houses. Most of them clustered around the harbour, but two very small isolated farms balanced one either side of the island on the slopes of the hill, while half-way up the hill, overlooking the harbour, the raggle-taggle of buildings where the shifting artist population lived, sprawled in the sunlight.

Almost hidden by its overgrown gardens and on its own, just beyond the end of the quay, was the house that Bethany had been waiting so anxiously to see. She hoped Nikolas wouldn't notice how misty her eyes were when she caught sight of it, and she felt a little disillusioned with Takis because he showed no sign of sharing her pleasure. Aunt Alexia's feelings were difficult to define, but when Bethany caught her eye for a moment and she smiled, Bethany thought she might be glad to be coming home too.

She wasn't quite sure by what means she had expected to return, but it had come as a surprise when Nikolas brought them himself in the same swift, luxurious craft he had taken them over in. Taking everything in to account, it was rather odd that she felt glad he had come too. As the buildings on land became more and more recognisable, she felt her heart beating hard and fast with excitement and stood on tiptoe so as not to miss a moment of this homecoming.

She darted a brief, almost defensive glance at Nikolas when she realised he was watching her, and she was never quite sure why she did it, but when their eyes met for a second, she smiled. 'Thank you,' she whispered, then hastily snatched her gaze back to the fast approaching shoreline and the familiar landmarks.

The fishing boats were still in harbour, for there was an hour or so yet until they would put out for the evening's fishing, and the men working in them looked up, acknowledging their arrival silently; dark eyes noting that the *xenos* had returned with them. Nikolas was viewed warily, Bethany guessed, not because he was a stranger, but because of the kind of man he was. But the judgment was not likely to be unfavourable, for he was caring for the family of Pavlos Meandis, and Pavlos had been well-liked. No one would have liked to see his family left to fend for themselves.

Takis was ashore first, taking the mooring line, then Nikolas assisted Alexia, leaving Bethany until last, and she could scarcely wait to set foot on her beloved island again. Holding tight to Nikolas's hand while he helped her ashore, she looked along the length of the quay, forgetting for the moment that she still clung to him.

'Are you happy now that you're back?' he asked, and she turned quickly to smile at him, her eyes shining.

'Oh, yes, Nikolas, I was so afraid that——'

'That I'd break my word?' He looked faintly amused, she thought, but she was in no mood to criticise him at the moment, and the slight pressure of his fingers reminded her that she was still holding his hand. Releasing her, he walked beside her in the direction of the house, following Takis and Alexia along the path from the quay. 'You didn't believe I'd bring you back, did you, Bethany?'

'Yes, of course I did, you promised!' She stopped herself there, because she remembered that he never actually promised; only her own conviction that he would had sustained her. 'Well, if you didn't actually promise, you gave me the impression that we'd come back.' She glanced ahead at Takis, hands thrust into his pockets and swaggering a little as if he felt himself much more important after a sojourn in the city.

'When Takis goes to his other school,' she ventured, 'what happens then, Nikolas?'

'Shall we wait and see?' he suggested, in a voice too quiet for either Takis or Alexia to have overheard.

Ahead of them, the old house looked frankly shabby in the sunlight, its paint peeling and the garden seeming more than ever like a jungle after the gardens in Rhodes. But Bethany loved it and, she told herself, she was never going to leave it, no matter what Nikolas decided; it was hers because Papa had willed it to her.

'The house is mine,' she reminded him. 'You said Papa left it to me, so I can stay here, Nikolas, if it's mine.'

Dark speculative eyes turned on her and for a moment the corners of his mouth curved upward in a hint of smile. 'Not quite as you put it, Bethany,' he said. 'Pavlos left the house as your dowry, but until you marry, your home depends on where I decide you shall live. I'm responsible for seeing that you're safely settled and that you come to no harm in the meantime. You know that, child, we've been through it all before.'

'And suppose I don't?' she asked, sounding a little breathless. 'I mean suppose I decide not to get married?'

She made the suggestion out of sheer bravado as they passed through the arched gateway and into the scented jungle she knew so well, and Nikolas shook his head as he opened the door and let the hot musty breath of emptiness out of the house. He admitted Alexia first, then ushered Bethany in behind her with an arm across her back, a touch that reminded her of the day at Kamiros when he had carried her down to his car. That rare, disturbing contact that had not been mentioned since.

'I think there's very little chance of you remaining unmarried,' he told her with confidence, and contemplated the big cool room thoughtfully for a moment. 'This is a good house, and a woman with such a dowry would have little difficulty in finding a husband, however undisciplined she was.' The dark eyes came back to her, deep and faintly mocking. 'Even less if she's young and very beautiful; lack of discipline can always be—remedied.'

'Nikolas!'

She stared at his back when he walked across to open a window and let in some fresh air as well as the hot, heady scents of the garden.

'Why do you have this fixed objection to marriage?' he asked, as if her answer was of little consequence and he merely asked out of casual curiosity. 'You're woman enough to have the normal feelings and needs, are you not?'

Bethany flushed warmly, thankful for the moment that he still had his back to her. 'That's neither here nor there,' she managed after a second or two. 'You said once that you knew who Papa had in mind for me to marry——'

'True, I do.'

'But you promised you wouldn't insist, if I was unwilling, whoever he is.' He nodded, breathing deeply at the open window and reacting as if he was still only superficially interested in the subject. 'You wouldn't go back on your word, would you?'

He looked back over his shoulder and the gleaming darkness of his eyes brought sudden urgency to her heartbeat. 'Do you think I would?' he challenged, and she shook her head, unable to do other than trust him.

Both Takis and Alexia seemed to have disappeared, so that they were alone when he came back to stand beside her. Without his actually touching her, his nearness sent little shivers of sensation fluttering over her skin, and she realised how much more familiar he had become in the few days they had been away. A realisation that was oddly disturbing.

'Then why not trust me?' he asked quietly.

She passed the tip of her tongue over her lips anxiously, then glanced upward. 'If you know who it is that Papa——'

'So that you can set your mind firmly against him?'

# Get your
# Harlequin Romance
## Home Subscription NOW!

## and get these 4 best-selling novels *FREE!*

Teachers Must Learn
NERINA HILLIARD

Cap Flamingo
VIOLET WINSPEAR

The Arrogant Duke
ANNE MATHER

Beyond the Sweet Waters
ANNE HAMPSON

# If you were in their place what would you do?

## Jeanette...

Though she has survived a heart-wrenching tragedy, is there more unhappiness in store for Jeanette? She is hopelessly in love with a man who is inaccessible to her. Her story will come alive in the pages of "Beyond the Sweet Waters" by Anne Hampson.

## Juliet...

Rather than let her father choose her husband, she ran...ran into the life of the haughty duke and his intriguing household on a Caribbean island. It's an intimate story that will stir you as you read "The Arrogant Duke" by Anne Mather.

## Laurel...

There was no turning back for Laurel. She was playing out a charade with the arrogant plantation owner, and the stakes were "love". It's all part of a thrilling romantic adventure called "Teachers Must Learn" by Nerina Hilliard.

## Fern...

She tried to escape to a new life...a new world...now she was faced with a loveless marriage of convenience. How long could she wait for the love she so strongly craved to come to her... Live with Fern... love with Fern...in the exciting "Cap Flamingo" by Violet Winspear.

Jeanette, Juliet, Laurel, Fern...these are some of the memorable people who come alive in the pages of Harlequin Romance novels. And now, without leaving your home, you can share their most intimate moments!

It's the easiest and most convenient way to get every one of the exciting Harlequin Romance novels! And now with a home subscription plan you won't miss *any* of these true-to-life stories, and you don't even have to go out looking for them.

# A Home Subscription! It's the easiest and most convenient way to get every one of the exciting Harlequin Romance Novels!

## ...and you'll get 4 of them FREE

You pay nothing extra for this convenience, there are no additional charges...you don't even pay for postage!

Fill out and send us the handy coupon now, and we'll send you 4 exciting Harlequin Romance novels absolutely FREE!

### Send no money, get these

## four books FREE

Mail this postpaid coupon today to:

### Harlequin Reader Service
### 901 Fuhrmann Blvd., Buffalo, N.Y. 14203

**YES,** please start a *Harlequin Romance* home subscription in my name, and send me FREE and without obligation my 4 *Harlequin Romances*. If you do not hear from me after I have examined my 4 FREE books, please send me the 6 new *Harlequin Romances* each month as soon as they come off the presses. I understand that I will be billed only $7.50 for all 6 books. There are no shipping and handling nor any other hidden charges. There is no minimum number of books that I have to purchase. In fact, I can cancel this arrangement at any time. The first 4 books are mine to keep as a FREE gift, even if I do not buy any additional books.

CR972

NAME

ADDRESS

CITY                    STATE                    ZIP CODE

This offer expires March 31, 1981. Prices subject to change without notice.
Offer not valid to present subscribers.

Printed in U.S.A.

## Get your
## *Harlequin Romance*
## Home Subscription NOW!

- Never miss a title!
- Get them first—straight from the presses!
- No additional costs for home delivery!
- These first 4 novels are yours FREE!

FIRST CLASS
PERMIT NO. 8907
Buffalo, N.Y.

## BUSINESS REPLY MAIL
No postage necessary if mailed in the United States.

Postage will be paid by

**Harlequin Reader Service
901 Fuhrmann Blvd.
Buffalo, N.Y. 14203**

Nikolas interrupted quietly. 'No, Bethany!' He looked over his shoulder at the open kitchen door where Alexia was already moving about preparing coffee for them. 'Hadn't you better give Aunt Alexia a hand with making the coffee?' he suggested. 'There are no servants here, as there were in Rodos.'

Bethany flushed, realising that things were back to normal as far as Nikolas was concerned. She was once more drawn back into the round of domestic chores, performed under his critical eye, and she flushed as she stepped around the pile of luggage containing hers and Takis's new clothes.

'I was just going to,' she told him, and thrust out her lower lip in reproach. 'You don't need to start hustling me around quite so soon, Nikolas!'

He said nothing at once, but caught her rebellious eye as she went into the kitchen to join Alexia, and one black brow winged upward. 'I won't unless I have to,' he promised.

Alexia looked pleased to see her, and from her smile Bethany again surmised that she was quite pleased to be back. 'You'll miss Rodos, Aunt Alexia?' she suggested, and Alexia's smile was gently non-committal.

'I've settled here,' she told her, which Bethany realised did not really confirm her pleasure. 'But you, child, you'll miss it, eh?'

Bethany could deny it with more certainty, and she did so unhesitatingly. 'I don't think so, Aunt Alex, I've been longing to come home. I missed Apolidus even more than I expected to.'

But however firmly she asserted it, Alexia's smile suggested she knew better, and as she put the coffee on to brew she watched Bethany set out a tray with cups and saucers and a dish of *loukoumi*. 'But you will surely miss your cousin Theo,' Alexia insisted, and inevitably she noted the flush that warmed Bethany's cheeks at the mention of him. 'He's so handsome and so charmin, isn't he? And very much taken with you, child, that was obvious.'

'Much to Nikolas's annoyance,' said Bethany, and

laughed a little wildly at the memory of Nikolas's dramatic arrival at Kamiros when he realised she and Theo were there alone—and his solemn warning about playing games with his impressionable brother. 'He didn't trust me alone with Theo, not even for a drive.'

'But naturally Niko is careful of your reputation,' Alexia told her, making it obvious that she was in agreement with him. 'He is a man of strict principles, and for you to be seen with a young man, even if he is to be your——' She caught her lip between her teeth and glanced at the kitchen door as if she feared being over heard, and Bethany stared at her.

She had a growing suspicion that Alexia had been about to give her the information that Nikolas consistently withheld. 'Aunt Alex?' Her heart banged urgently at her ribs. 'If Theo is to be—what, Aunt Alex?'

'Bethany, child.' Quite obviously she regretted having betrayed something she was meant to keep to herself, but equally obviously Bethany's expression convinced her it wouldn't be allowed to rest there, in fact she probably felt she would be pleasing her by passing on the news. 'I have reason to believe that the man your papa wished you to marry is your cousin Theo.' Seeing the way Bethany looked she frowned at her curiously. 'Would it be such a dreadful thing, child?' she insisted. 'Theo is handsome and charming, and many young women would envy you.'

Bethany thought it quite possible, but there were other, even more discomfiting possibilities troubling her at the moment. 'What makes you say it's Theo that Papa had in mind, Aunt Alex?' she asked. 'Did—did someone tell you?'

She knew instinctively that Theo with his taste for good living and innumerable girl-friends would die of boredom in Apolidus, and she did not yet stop to think that if she loved him enough she would willingly go wherever he was. Quite inexplicably, it was not Theo who had prior place in her thoughts at the moment, but Nikolas.

Alexia looked unhappy, as if she would rather not have said any more on the subject. 'Something Nikolas said,' she admitted, and Bethany shook her head impatiently.

'Nikolas!'

Very clearly Alexia felt herself in a predicament, and if Nikolas had confided the news in confidence, Bethany could understand her feelings. Nikolas had announced that if it was at all possible, he would see that her stepfather's wishes were complied with, but somehow the prospect had seemed too far in the future to be taken seriously. Now it seemed it was all too close at hand, and she took a moment or two to absorb the fact.

There were too many disturbing recollections running through her mind, ones she did not care to dwell on, but which thrust themselves to the forefront of her mind as she coped with the unexpected. Right from the beginning Nikolas had determinedly set about changing her into a different kind of woman, and she had simply resented it without really looking for a reason.

It had never for a moment occurred to her conscious mind that he was making the changes for his own benefit, but every instinct rebelled against the idea of him doing it for his brother's, and the truth hurt like a blow; the more because it was unexpected.

She recalled his generosity in buying her new clothes, and the uncharacteristically gentle way he had explained how he was trying to make a flesh and blood woman of her—a Meandis for preference. How he had snatched her away from Theo at Kamiros and threatened what he would do if she ever behaved towards his brother as she had with him. And all because he was preparing to hand her over, suitably subdued and obedient, to become Theo's wife.

She could recall too easily the warm comfort of his body and the hard, steady beat of his heart when he held her close after her fall, and the feel of being carried in his arms, and she suddenly felt almost physically sick. 'He's—he's preparing me,' she whispered in a huskily choked voice. 'He's making sure I—I don't disappoint his brother! He doesn't—he never has cared what or how I feel!'

'Oh, Bethany!' Alexia looked shocked, and once more she glanced at the doorway uneasily. 'You mustn't judge him so harshly, child.'

'Oh, I can judge Nikolas perfectly!' Bethany assured her bitterly. 'He knows exactly what a Meandis bride should be like, and he means to make sure I come up to standard, however he achieves it!'

'Bethany, no!'

'Yes!' Bethany insisted, the hurt deep inside her driving her on. 'Yes, yes, yes! He isn't doing it for my sake, all this—this training, or for some mysterious bridegroom that Papa chose for me, not even for himself!' That, she found, hurt most of all, and she laughed without humour, a wild, half-hysterical sound as she shook her head. 'Never mind how promiscuous the bridegroom might be, he's a Meandis so he has to have a suitable bride! No artist's brat for a Meandis, but someone personally trained and approved by the head man himself!'

Alexia looked blankly shocked, but for the moment Bethany was beyond caring who she hurt or distressed. She clenched her hands tightly, and tears trembled in her eyes, because all she could think of was that Nikolas did not see her as a woman in her own right, but merely as a suitable bride for his brother—once he had knocked all the rough edges off her, of course.

A sound of movement in the living-room made her turn sharply. The situation was unbearable enough without being faced with Nikolas's sudden appearance. Now that she had her bitterness off her chest, it began to dawn on her just how virulent she had been, and it was as much because she realised at last how much she had disturbed Alexia that she acted as she did.

'If you don't mind, Aunt Alex, I'd like to go away and think about this—I—I need to think.'

Alexia was appealing to her, alarmed at the fever of emotion she had aroused. 'I shouldn't have told you,' she said, her soft voice dull with regret. 'Please don't blame Niko too much, Bethany, he's doing what he thinks is right.'

Bethany twisted her mouth into a parody of a smile. 'Oh, I don't really blame him, I suppose,' she said. 'Nikolas is just running true to form; I'm just not—I've just never met anyone like him before, and I____'

She shook her head, darting a swift glance over her shoulder when Nikolas's firm and unmistakable tread came nearer the kitchen door. She turned and half ran across the kitchen, brushing past Nikolas in the doorway, but ignoring his call as she went through the living-room and made for the door.

Without pausing for breath, she hurried through the garden, ducking under the overgrown shrubs and through the gate to the path that led to the harbour. Not even the new shoes that pinched her feet as she crossed the cobbled quay slowed her down, though they made her wince with pain. Already she regretted saying most of the things she had said to Alexia, but being sorry didn't make her any less resentful of his deviousness, and in her present state of confusion anything was better than facing Nikolas.

Heedless of the direction she was taking, she climbed the hill above the harbour purely by instinct, and made, not for the art colony, but for a deep, secret hollow on the west side of the hill where she had been often with Takis. It was where they had their very minor dig that Nikolas insisted was illegal, and she could be sure of being alone there, with time and opportunity to think.

Evening was drawing in, but the sun was still hot enough to have made her feel overheated and sticky, and she sank thankfully on to the cool ground on the lip of the hollow. She tried hard to think clearly and constructively, but always she came back to the fact that Nikolas was taking advantage of his situation as her guardian to treat her shamefully, and she would find it hard to forgive him.

She did not for a moment doubt that Alexia had her facts right, and that Nikolas had given her a clue about Papa's choice of a husband for her. To give Theo his due, he would probably be much less concerned by her behaviour, but Nikolas was guardian of the family name and honour, and in a position to train her to the standards he considered were required in a Meandis wife.

'Like a performing horse, or a puppet on a string!'

She thumped the ground either side of her in fury and frustration, and railed inwardly against her own foolishness for wanting to weep when she remembered those gentler moments that Nikolas was capable of. In his way he was as charming and seductive as Theo was, perhaps more so, and he was certainly much more dangerous.

The new shoes were still making her feet hurt so she pulled them off, holding them in her hands for a moment while she recalled who their donor was. Then she flung them from her in a sudden spasm of rage and despair, watching them tumble down into the hollow, where they lay smart and incongruous on the churned red soil where she and Takis had been digging.

'That's a very expensive gesture!' She turned swiftly and just managed to conceal the disappointment she felt that it wasn't Nikolas who stood just behind her with his face in the shadows and his back to the lowering sun. 'Shall I be intruding if I join you?' the man asked.

He indicated a spot next to her and Bethany nodded automatically, a vague sense of anticipation making her eye him curiously as he sat down beside her. It was only when he turned his face into the sun and she could see his features more distinctly that she realised who he was, and her heart gave a sudden and unexpected lurch. For almost certainly the man who settled himself on the ground next to her was the same one she had noticed on two other occasions—at the harbour in Rhodes and at Kamiros.

He was tall, and lean to the point of gauntness, and his hands when he clasped them around his knees were long and bony. But it was his face that was so strikingly familiar, and she looked at him covertly for as long as she dared without making it obvious. He definitely was one of the artists from the commune on the hill, for unmistakably the faint colour on one leg of his light slacks was a partially washed-out paint stain.

He was handsome, almost incredibly so for a man of his years, for he must have been nearing fifty, and in profile his features were classical in their clear-cut perfection, just as her own were. He turned his head and smiled at her, as if he was, after all, aware of her interest, and she noticed that his brow was high and smooth and his nose straight and perfectly proportioned. The mouth was full and definitely sensual, but again classically perfect, and slightly thinning hair swept back in two wings of light brown from a centre parting. Bethany could not imagine where she had seen him before, and yet the haunting familiarity still persisted.

He indicated her abandoned shoes with a tilt of his head, but there was nothing censorious in the brown eyes, rather they seemed faintly amused. 'Have you got something against those shoes?' he asked, and Bethany glanced at him from the corner of her eye before she answered him.

'They hurt,' she told him. 'And they're not really me, they're—town shoes.'

'Expensive ones, I would say.'

They looked rather pathetic lying down there in the rubble, Bethany realised, and remembered how pleased she had been with them when they were bought. The recollection made her uneasy, so she shrugged as if the expense did not matter, unwilling to even hint that a sudden unreasoning hatred of the man who had bought them for her was the reason she rejected them.

Quite accidentally she caught his eye for a moment,

and the look she saw there sent a curious little shiver of sensation slipping along her spine. 'I'll collect them before I go home,' she said, as if it was of little consequence.

Although she had again shifted her gaze to the shoes lying down in the bottom of the hollow, she thought the man still watched her closely. He plucked a stem of the sparse, sun-scorched grass and pushed it into his mouth, gnawing at the hard stalk while he spoke. 'I would guess that somebody's upset you, am I right?'

Bethany coloured slightly, confirming what she was reluctant to admit verbally. 'Oh, just a family misunderstanding,' she allowed, and wondered how she could sound so cool about it, when she had just fled the house in a blind fury at Nikolas's behaviour. Glancing again at his teasingly familiar face, she took the bull by the horns. 'I have a feeling I know you,' she said, and went on hastily, 'I don't know your name, but I just have a feeling I should know you from somewhere.'

'I noticed you in Rhodes,' he told her, unexpectedly frank. 'And you were at Kamiros with——'

'My cousin,' Bethany assured him hastily, in case he held some of the same views as Nikolas, although she doubted it somehow.

'Your cousin?' Fine pale brows almost suggested he was in some doubt of it, and Bethany flushed. 'He's very good-looking.'

'He is,' she confirmed, but sidestepped the subject of Theo to pursue one that interested her more at the moment. 'Are you from the commune? Are you an artist?'

A smile dismissed any suggestion that her curiosity offended him, but he had probably spent enough time with Greeks to have become accustomed to the national trait of a people who take an interest in anyone and everyone's private life. 'Yes to both questions!'

It occurred to Bethany then that she had automatically assumed he was a foreign national living in Greece, like most of the members of the commune. But very few of them spoke Greek, and this man spoke it well and with only a very slight accent. 'You speak very good Greek,' she ventured, and laughed a little awkwardly as she plunged on. 'I know you aren't Greek because you have an accent of some kind, but it's hardly noticeable. And you said Rhodes, not Rodos as a Greek would.'

He inclined his head in a mock half-bow, and his rather fine eyes seemed to be smiling at her again. 'I'm flattered,' he told her, then one brow winged upward curiously. 'But unless I'm very wrong, you have no accent at all and *you're* not Greek, are you?'

It was instinctive to put a hand to her tawny hair, and she shook her head. 'Actually I'm part Welsh.'

'Do you speak any English?'

The sudden change of language put her at a disadvantage for a second, but she recovered quickly and answered in the tongue that Papa had made sure she never forgot. 'Yes; Papa made sure I always practised when he was alive. My stepfather,' she hastened to explain in a voice suddenly grown slightly husky. 'He died only a short time ago.'

'And you loved him very much.'

It was a statement of fact, not a question, and Bethany nodded unhesitatingly. 'He was a wonderful man, and I loved him dearly.' For a moment she wondered why the words sounded so much more trite spoken in English, and decided that she had become a stranger to her own tongue. 'I've lived in Greece for most of my life,' she went on, reverting again to Greek because she felt more at ease with it. 'I've lived here in Apolidus since I was six or seven. I love it, there's nowhere else like it.'

The clear, straight profile was turned to her and short light lashes shadowed the man's eyes as he gazed downward into the hollow instead of looking directly at her as he had been. 'You don't remember your own father?' he asked, and Bethany shook her head firmly.

She answered the question unwillingly as she always did, but somehow it did not occur to her not to answer it. 'I don't remember my father; I was five when I saw him last, and I doubt if he cares any more now if I'm alive or dead than he did then.'

'Argh!'

It was a curious sound he made in his throat, but Bethany had never sought pity for the loss of her own father; only Papa had ever mattered to her. Hugging her knees close, she too gazed down into the hollow at her discarded shoes, making the rather fanciful comparison in her mind, that her father had thrown away his right to her love as carelessly as she had discarded her shoes.

'I have sometimes wondered what he was like,' she confessed, and paused for a moment to consider why it was that she was discussing with this stranger, a subject that she normally avoided. Seeking a diversion, she turned and looked at him again, once more teased by the familiarity of his features, but no nearer to solving the puzzle. 'How long have you been with the commune?' she asked.

'A little while.' He smiled, looking at her thoughtfully. 'Just—checking up on old acquaintances, that's all. I'm moving on tonight; taking the evening ferry to Piraeus. It's a habit I have,' he explained, and laughed. 'I move on whenever I feel I'm beginning to take root.'

It was a feeling Bethany did not begin to understand. 'You don't want a home? A family?'

'I never have,' he told her, and glanced at the watch that encircled his wrist. 'There's nothing I have that anyone would want, and I've never taken to the domestic scene. And I'd better be off if I'm to get the ferry.'

Bethany checked the time on her own watch, realising how his presence had distracted her from her earlier unhappiness, and reluctant to lose his companionship. 'You've time yet,' she told him. 'It doesn't go for another two hours.'

Quite clearly he was anxious to be away, and Bethany wondered if her questions about settling down with a family had embarrassed him after all. 'Things to do,' he said as he got up, but he stood for a moment looking down at her, and when she started to get up too, he took both her hands and helped her up. 'You're a very pretty child,' he said. 'Are you called by a Greek name as pretty as you are?'

It was a curious way to have worded it, Bethany thought, but he was perhaps less familiar with the language than he seemed. 'I'm Bethany,' she told him. 'Bethany Meandis. I kept my first name when Papa adopted me.'

'Ah!' It was odd that he sounded so satisfied about it, but Bethany found him an intriguing man altogether, and she was sorry to see him go. 'I hope one of your family comes to find you soon, before it grows dark,' he said, 'you're much too lovely to be abandoned on a hillside.' He proffered a hand in parting. 'I'm very glad I saw you, Bethany Meandis.'

She shook his hand and smiled, even though his mention of someone coming to find her reminded her of the reason she was there. 'I hope you have a good journey to—wherever you go.'

He seemed to hesitate briefly, then turned and started down the hill towards the commune in long quick strides that suggested impatience. He was several metres below her when Bethany realised that she still did not know his name, and she called after him impulsively, still plagued by that haunting sense of familiarity.

'You didn't tell me your name!'

The man turned and looked up at her where she stood slim and golden against the evening sky, then he smiled, a slow, crooked and slightly bitter smile that troubled her without reason. 'Apollo,' he called back. 'I'm called Apollo! Goodbye, little one—be happy!'

Be happy, the ancient Greek blessing. Strangely disturbed by him, Bethany watched the man who so appropriately called himself Apollo go on down the hill, then she turned away when he disappeared into the commune, and sighed deeply. She was feeling sorry for herself, she realised, but no matter how she tried to think sensibly about Nikolas her emotions always got the better of her and she found herself angry with him all over again.

The sun was going down when she decided to walk down the other side of the hill to the sea, the virtually uninhabited side of the island, where the swimming was safe, and it was quiet and peaceful, with only one small farmhouse perched up in the arable land above the sea. It was a favourite place of hers and Takis's, although Takis would probably scorn such simple delights now that he had had a taste of a more sophisticated way of life. And she blamed Nikolas for that too; Takis would have been content if he had not been shown the kind of life his newly found family enjoyed.

The sea had always enchanted her and she stood at the water's edge, reminded briefly of her discarded shoes when she realised her stockinged feet were getting wet. To remove them and walk along the water's edge with her bare feet was an unconscious gesture of defiance, but the setting and the soft ripple of the tide around her ankles was soothing, and before she reached the cove that she and Takis had often swum from, she felt much more relaxed and easy.

Bethany did not remember having been taught to swim, but she could remember teaching Takis when he was quite small, and they had always enjoyed it. She saw no reason why the lack of a swimming costume should inhibit her, since there was no one else about, nor was there likely to be. She knew the cove well, and no one ever came there but her and Takis.

Stripping off her few clothes, she stretched luxuriously in the silky cool breeze that caressed her skin, then plunged into the sea at almost the exact same moment as the sun descended into it. For a while the sky was a vast canvas of crimson and gold, changing rapidly to amethyst and purple and staining the rocks on land with the same rich gamut of colours, and Bethany felt a wonderful sense of oneness with the warm dark ocean. Sweeping one slim arm after the

other in lazy arcs, she swam further out to sea before
turning to move easily along the shoreline.

The moon followed closely on the heels of the dying
sun, and its appearance, Bethany judged, made it time
to relinquish the quiet soothing peace of the sea for
the harsher reality of Nikolas's anger. She had little
doubt that by now he would be angry about her ab-
sence, but secretly she nurtured a hope that he would
feel a little concerned too. It did not even occur to her
that Aunt Alexia might be concerned, for Alexia was
accustomed to such unconventional behaviour and accepted it. But to Nikolas such impulsive gestures
would be as foreign as so many other aspects of their
life-style were.

She was already part way out of the water, and sub-
merged only as far as her waist, when she realised that
someone was standing on the white-sanded beach, and
instinctively she crossed her arms over her breasts,
clasping the tops of her arms and catching at her
breath. A tall, dark and vaguely ominous figure stood
between her and the spot where she had left her
clothes, and she had no doubt at all that it was Nikolas.

The moon was less than full, but even so she could
swear that the dark gleam of his eyes was discernible,
and she shivered. Not because it was chill, but because
the moment seemed to be somehow suspended in time
and pregnant with the violence of emotions she could
not even begin to recognise. He could have moved
away, she thought wildly, but instead he simply stood
looking at her from the very edge of the tide, pale and
slender as she stood with the sea lapping about her;
tossing back thick strands of hair that clung wetly to
the golden creaminess of her skin, and too stunned
for the moment to seek the concealment of the water.

'Nikolas.' She called to him softly, but her voice
died on the light warm wind without reaching him.
'Please move away.' She called louder now because he
made no move to show he understood. 'My clothes are
just behind you!'

He half turned his head then, and she could imagine his expression, even though she couldn't actually see it. He would look as he so often did; dark and disturbingly fierce, his mouth set hard and straight and his eyes glittering between their thick lashes. Angry, as he so often was with her. Then he glanced in the other direction, to where a cluster of trees overhung some rocks, and he pointed a hand at them.

'Go along there,' he directed; and when she hesitated. 'Do as I say, girl!'

He actually waited until she turned and slid back into the water before he went to fetch her clothes, as if he did not trust her to obey. As if she had much option, she thought a little wildly, when she was as naked as a new-born babe and had nowhere to go but back with him. He would find her clothes easily enough, she knew, but as she emerged once more from the water she wished her moment of freedom could have had a happier ending.

His back was to her as she slipped across the warm white sand and into the concealment of the rocks, but she was shivering now and her heart beat so rapidly that her whole body seemed to quiver with its urgency as she listened for him coming. Her footprints showed as small darker hollows in the sand and her skin had a translucent paleness in the moonlight, so that she felt strangely exposed, despite the concealing rocks and once more placed her arms across her breast while she waited.

She could see nothing over the top, and she caught her breath audibly when, after what seemed like an interminable time, a hand appeared holding not only the few brief garments she had been wearing, but her abandoned shoes as well. She stared at them for a second, until the hand shook impatiently, and Nikolas's voice dragged her out of her surprised silence.

'Take them,' he ordered, 'and get dressed, quickly!'

She did as he said automatically, murmuring her thanks. But she had nothing with which to dry herself, and dressing a wet body was horribly uncomfortable, nor did it help that she knew how impatiently he would be waiting for her. She drew the line at putting on the too-tight shoes, however, and stepped out from behind the rocks carrying one in each hand.

Nikolas was standing with his arms folded and leaned against one of the rocks, much closer than she had realised, and she found it quite inexplicable when her first instinct was to reach out and touch him. For the moment Bethany stayed out of his line of vision, although it was unlikely that he could be unaware of her being there.

'How did you find me?' she ventured when he made no move, and he turned his head so suddenly that she blinked, half expecting some physical reaction, although he had never struck her yet.

'I sent Takis first.' His voice still had that grating harshness she had noted earlier. 'He couldn't see anything of you, but some man told him that he'd seen you up on the hill.'

Bethany was nodding, recalling the spoken hope of the man that someone would soon come and find her. 'Was he catching the ferry?' she asked, and Nikolas eyed her narrowly.

'You know him?'

She blinked rapidly at the sharpness of his tone, then shook her head slowly. 'Not really. I've seen him a couple of times before, and when he found me up there by our dig, he—we talked for a while.'

Dark eyes raked over her searingly, glinting like jet in the paleness of moonlight. 'Who is he, Bethany?'

The clinging dampness of her dress made her feel she was still naked under that harsh scrutiny, and she held tight to her seething emotions. 'I don't know.' She made the confession unwillingly. 'He—he calls himself Apollo.'

'Holy Saint Peter!' His pious oath was blatantly at odds with the gleaming darkness of his eyes, and Bethany's heart began its urgent tattoo again; neither angry nor afraid, but some curious mingling of emotions bringing warm high colour to her cheeks. 'When Takis came back to say he couldn't see you at your dig, as the man had said, I didn't know what to expect! Have you no sense at all, girl, that you go wandering off alone without telling anyone where you're going? Meeting a strange man!'

It was anger, Bethany felt sure, that made her turn on him as she did, but there was a curiously heady feeling about it too. 'We talked,' she insisted in a husky voice. 'That's all, we just talked for a few moments!' She met his eyes for a moment and challenged him to find cause for complaint in her few minutes' conversation with the man whose features still lingered tauntingly in her mind's eye. 'You don't have to look so disapproving, Nikolas! He wasn't like that.'

'How do you know?' Nikolas countered harshly, and she recalled uneasily a certain look in the man's eyes that had given her a moment's misgiving.

'Because—I know!' she insisted.

Nikolas's eyes gleamed darkly at her, his features almost satanically strong and dark in the moonlight. 'Did you play your provoking little games with him?' he rasped. 'Is that how you're so sure?'

'Nikolas!'

She stared at him unbelievingly, but he seemed sunk in some deep uneasy reverie of his own. 'Holy Mother! When I saw your shoes lying down there, and the earth disturbed, I thought for a moment——'

'Oh, Nikolas, no!' Bethany spoke softly, understanding at last and chokingly close to tears when she realised what must have been going on in his mind when he came in search of her. 'I forgot about the shoes. I threw them down there because they hurt, and I was angry—oh, I don't know!' She moved round in front of him, trying to get a clearer look at the dark, fierce face. 'I'd no idea you'd think something had happened to me.'

'Didn't it even occur to you?' She shook her head, avoiding his eyes because they were bound to condemn her. 'Then to see someone in the water—to find you swimming, naked as a harlot and without a care in the world!'

'You've called me that before!' Her own anger rose, sparked by the injustice of it, but it was an exciting kind of anger that brought a rapid urgent beat to her heart and made the blood sing through her veins. 'I really think you'd like to believe it of me, wouldn't you, Nikolas?'

Once more his eyes raked over her body in clinging damp cotton, and unconsciously she drew herself up, tossing back her hair that still clung in damp tendrils to her neck and shoulders. 'I *won't* believe it,' he said in a quiet, firm voice. 'But I'll make sure you realise what impression you give by behaving as you do!'

'I'm not in the habit of swimming naked,' Bethany insisted. 'And no one saw me!'

'You're wrong,' Nikolas corrected her sharply. '*I* saw you!'

Bethany had never felt quite as she did at that moment, although she had come close to it that day at Kamiros, when she had found the need to challenge him irresistible. 'Then I'm lucky it wasn't Theo,' she countered huskily. 'You're much less susceptible to temptation than he is, aren't you, Niko?' She rarely used the affectionate abbreviation of his name, and she was vaguely shocked to realise that she did so now quite deliberately.

'Stop it, Bethany!'

'But of course it wouldn't do for you to try taking advantage of the woman you're training to be——' She bit back hastily before she betrayed the fact that Alexia had been indiscreet about his plans for her. She did not want to upset relations between him and Alexia, for Alexia's sake. 'Not,' she went on anxious to conceal her original meaning, 'that I really believe what Theo said about your liking for women—you're not the type!'

'Will you be quiet!' He turned her about roughly and began the climb up the steep hill; dark and lonely where the trees clustered, and starkly shadowed away from them. Nikolas's hand gripped her arm so hard that his strong hard fingers dug into her flesh and betrayed his anger as surely as the harshness of his voice did. 'You provoke me beyond endurance at times, and I shan't warn you again, Bethany! You don't realise the kind of situation your teasing could give rise to.' Turning his head suddenly he looked down at her, his eyes raking the pale oval of her face. 'I *hope* you don't realise it; if I thought you did——'

Bethany turned up her face to him and her eyes were two huge shiny orbs between smudges of darker lashes, her lips parted and half smiling in defiance of his anger. A strange new excitement drove her on, making her forget how she had hated him when she fled from the house earlier. It tingled through her whole body, a sense of power that she could neither explain nor wished to at the moment.

'If I did, Niko?' she prompted, and the sound of his breath came in a great shuddering sigh as he reached out for her.

She was drawn against him with a hard fierce pull that almost knocked the breath from her, and bound to him with arms that made no allowances for the soft vulnerability of her body. One hand gripped the nape of her neck, twisting painfuly in her damp hair, and her head was forced back by the violence of his mouth on hers. For several moments it seemed she had stopped breathing, and although her body shrank from the bruising force of him, her senses clamoured for the wild excitement of his mouth.

He raised his head and looked down into her eyes for a long moment, the hand on her neck sliding down to press into the small of her back as its mate did, and he was breathing fast and unevenly with his lips slightly apart. Then he thrust her from him suddenly, and moved away, running both hands over his hair and keeping his face averted when he spoke.

'Did I hurt you?' Too shaken to reply, Bethany merely shook her head, and he turned, looking at her with narrowed eyes for a moment before he spoke again. 'You see how dangerous it is to—behave as you do?'

She shook her head. Her mouth tingled still and it

was quite unconscious when she put her fingers to her lips and lightly brushed them. But there was one point she had to put him right on, and it did not yet occur to her what the implication of her words were. 'I don't behave—like that,' she denied. 'Not with anyone else, Nikolas.'

It was so difficult to see what his reaction was, for he still stood away from her a little, and the dimness of moonlight made shadows on his face when he turned it in profile to her again. She was growing cool in her wet clothes, even though the wind was warm, and she shivered slightly; a small enough gesture but one that Nikolas noticed.

'You're cold?' He scanned her slender shape with the thin cotton dress clinging to damp skin, and he extended a hand to her. 'Come, let's go home and you can change into dry clothes.'

He was the authoritative guardian again, and Bethany did not like the reversion. 'I'm all right,' she told him, ignoring the hand he held out. 'And I'm not cold, it's just the——'

She had been about to say it was because he had been holding her in his arms, inducing a glowing warmth in her that she missed now that he again kept his distance, but she shook her head. Nikolas was not so easily denied, however, and he still held his hand out to her, the long brown fingers curved invitingly.

'Come home,' he said, soft-voiced, and without further hesitation Bethany succumbed to their persuasion and took his hand. Neither of them noticed for the moment that her shoes had once more been abandoned and forgotten somewhere on the hillside.

# CHAPTER SIX

IT was nearly two weeks after Bethany had taken her moonlight swim and ended the evening with startling unexpectedness in Nikolas's arms, but she was still plagued by an inexplicable restlessness. A curious sense of anticipation that persisted even though nothing had changed superficially. It was simply that she found it much harder to sit at table with him, or to be in the same room for any length of time without feeling a strange sense of unrest she had never known before.

Apolidus had provided her with everything she needed for as long as she could remember, but now suddenly she felt a need for something more, without having the least idea what it was she wanted. It was that same restlessness that sent her in search of isolation one morning after she and Alexia had finished the baking, and it was quite unplanned when she found herself once more by the dig that had been abandoned ever since Papa died.

She sat for a while gazing down at the bright dazzle of the ocean and thinking about the last time she was there, when she had been joined by the man who called himself Apollo, and suddenly something clicked into place. She thought she knew why those classically handsome features had struck her as so persistently familiar, and she could scarcely wait to prove it to herself.

The problem was that the evidence she needed was once more covered over by the debris of a minor landslide that had happened since their last visit. It had brought down a heap of sandy red earth and small boulders that she found impossible to move with her bare hands, which was why she had returned to the house by a shorter back way that took her past the studio window.

Since Nikolas needed to keep in touch with his business concerns, he occasionally used the studio as an office, and Bethany scarcely noticed if he was there or not as she went hurrying by the open window. But she was not left long in doubt when her name was called in a voice there was no mistaking.

'Bethany!'

She came to a halt and heaved a massive sigh of resignation that he could hardly have missed, as she swung round to face him. He stood at the open window looking vaguely menacing, as he sometimes did to her prejudiced eye, and he took swift note of the dust liberally spattered over her dark blue dress and clinging to her hands. He was frowning, which was inevitable, she supposed, but lately she had felt rather less disposed towards coming into open conflict with him, which was why she simply stood and waited for him to make the first move.

'What on earth happened to you?'

She shook her head, optimistically denying anything had happened because she was unwilling to confide in him at the moment. 'Nothing's happened, Nikolas. We've finished baking and Aunt Alex didn't need me for anything else just yet, so I went for a walk.' It dawned on her then how meticulously she was spelling it out for him and she shook herself impatiently. When she looked at him again, it was a quite deliberately provocative glance. 'You don't *mind* my going for a walk, do you, Nikolas?'

'Not in the least,' he answered coolly but there was an edge of harshness on his voice that she took heed of. 'I'm your guardian, Bethany, not your jailor.'

'Then if you'll excuse me——'

'Have you had an accident? You can't expect me to believe you got into that state simply by going for a walk,' he pointed out impatiently. 'What happened to you? *Did* you have an accident?'

'No, I'm all right.'

She should have been grateful for his concern, she told herself. If it had been her stepfather showing such consideration she would have reacted quite differently, but it wasn't the same at all with Nikolas. She retraced a couple of steps until she stood by the window, wishing she did not again experience those discomfiting variations in her heartbeat when she caught his eye for a moment.

'I went as far as the dig,' she explained, 'and I've got a bit dirty, but I need some tools, so I had to——'

'Tools?' Telling him that had been a mistake, she realised, but it was too late to retract, and she stepped back hastily when he suddenly swung his long legs over the sill. As he stood beside her on the path, his eyes narrowed slightly. 'Bethany, what exactly are you doing?'

'Nothing!'

She was insistent, but obviously not very convincing, for Nikolas gave an exasperated sigh that somehow turned into a snort of disbelief, and he placed both hands on his hips as he stood facing her. 'Don't lie to me, you maddening little wretch!' he ordered sternly. 'What do you need tools for? You're not trying to excavate that dig of yours again, are you? I've told you it's illegal without a permit, and I know you don't have one.'

'But it could take weeks, months, even years for an official party to come here;' Bethany protested, and her face was warmly flushed as she fought against his logic as well as his authority. 'You know it would, Nikolas!'

'And you're in a hurry?'

She lifted her shoulders, uneasy about trying to explain her reasons. 'I just don't want to wait until some fuddy-duddy old professor decides to come and find it, that's all.'

'It?'

She shrugged again uneasily, seeing herself led inexorably in a direction she would much rather not go. 'Takis and I found a bust of Apollo,' she told him reluctantly. 'It isn't enough to make a lot of fuss about, Nikolas.'

'Tell me about it!'

Bethany took a sideways glance at him, almost believing that she might have convinced him. His expression gave little away, except that he was growing impatient, and she passed a moist tongue over her lips before she began. 'You remember that man I told you I'd spoken with at the dig the night you——' She broke off, unwilling to remind him of the way that evening had ended. 'You remember?'

'I remember,' Nikolas assured her quietly, but his eyes were narrowed and his mouth had that tight look she so disliked. 'I understood the man had left the island that night. If he's back, Bethany, and——'

'He isn't,' she interrupted swiftly. 'I'm trying to explain, Nikolas, if only you'll listen!' He nodded abruptly, though obviously he was already biased, and Bethany wished she had a more sympathetic listener. 'When we arrived in Rodos,' she went on, 'I noticed a man standing over by the market and looking at— he seemed to be looking at us. Then I saw him again at Kamiros, although Theo was convinced I was seeing things. He's—haunted me.'

She chose the word with care, and realised it was the only one that aptly described the feeling the man's uncanny familiarity had given her. But Nikolas was frowning again. 'And it was the same man you saw that evening—the one you spoke with?'

Bethany nodded. 'The one who told Takis where I was, or rather where he'd seen me last. I told you he called himself Apollo, if you remember.' He nodded, still impatient for her to come to the point. 'Well, he *is* Apollo, Nikolas.' She laughed a little unsteadily because she still found it a little hard to believe in the uncanny resemblance herself. 'That's why I want to dig out the bust of the marble Apollo; to make sure I haven't made a mistake. I *know* I haven't made a mistake, but it's so incredible I can still hardly believe it. That man is exactly like the marble head, it's—it's uncanny!'

'Bethany——'

He seemed uncertain, and that in itself was encour-

agement enough where Nikolas was concerned, so that
Bethany took it as a sign of weakening and hastened to
reinforce her argument. 'I can't wait for all the official
red tape to set things in motion,' she pleaded. 'It's
nothing I can't move quite easily myself, Nikolas,
there's been a slight landslide inside the dig, but——'

'Then leave it alone!' he instructed. 'Apart from
anything else it's too dangerous to go excavating,
you'll probably bring down more if you start disturbing the lower slope.'

'Oh, but I'm sure it wouldn't!'

'Leave it alone, Bethany!' His dark eyes had a narrowed intensity that was hard to defy, and after a
second or two she lowered her own eyes, but her hands
were clenched and she felt bitterly frustrated at being
so firmly forbidden. 'If you really think this sculpture
is worth recovering,' Nikolas went on, 'I'll notify the
proper authorities and they can do whatever they think
necessary.' Bethany said nothing, there was nothing
she could say that she would not regret later. 'You
surely don't really believe this?' he asked after a moment or two. 'A man the exact image of an Apollo
carved—heaven knows how many years ago? You must
know it doesn't make sense, Bethany.'

'If you'd seen him, you'd know,' Bethany insisted,
but he was shaking his head impatiently.

'For heaven's sake, child, the gods don't walk the
earth, whatever the old myths say! I allow that there
might be a passing resemblance between the man you
saw and the bust of Apollo you found, but the rest is
fancy.'

Bethany clenched her hands and glared at him,
ignoring the colloquial use and taking the word child
in its literal sense. 'I'm not a child,' she informed him
clearly and distinctly, 'and I'm not making this up,
Nikolas. When I've recovered the Apollo you'll see,
Takis will bear me out; he spoke to him.'

'That dig will not be touched again,' Nikolas declared with equal clarity, 'until someone more quali-

fied comes to unearth whatever it is you've found. And
that is final, Bethany!'

He stressed the last few words in a firm, hard voice
when she opened her mouth to argue with him, and
Bethany heaved a loud and very elaborate sigh when
she yielded. But as she walked away from him she felt
a curious sense of hurt because he had failed to understand how she felt. She had once told him that he
would never understand her, and despite the hope she
had nurtured lately that she might be wrong, this
latest gesture made it all too clear that she had been
right.

She did not even bother to see what he did or where
he went, but went on through the garden, an unaccustomed stiffness in her stance and clenching her
hands tightly. She could so easily uncover the thing
herself without causing further falls of earth and rocks,
and he had been quite unreasonable about it. By the
time she had made her way to the little stone outhouse
where the tools were kept, she had convinced herself
it was worth a try, and that he couldn't really do anything about stopping her.

Only a few minutes later she set off for the dig once
more, with the necessary tools, and taking the long
way around so that she need not pass the studio window again, for she didn't think she had the necessary
nerve to defy him openly. If necessary she could cover
the Apollo up again and with luck Nikolas need never
know. It was annoying to realise that she felt guilty
about deceiving him, but she consoled her uneasy conscience with the thought that if he never found out it
wouldn't matter.

Nevertheless she glanced quite frequently over her
shoulder on the return journey, and she supposed her
conscience was less easily quieted than she had hoped.
Climbing the western slope of the hill again the dig
loomed like a dark scar in the hillside, lower on the
ocean side and soaring steeply on the landward side, a
long red gash of loose earth and stones that occasionally shifted and slid downwards into the hollow.

But a further slide was not even in her mind as she approached the dig, for she could see below her the beach where Nikolas had found her nearly two weeks before, and the sight of it gave her another moment of regret at deceiving him. It was much too easy to remember how she had stood on this same hillside in the moonlight while Nikolas kissed her in such a way that she had not even known what time it was. Nikolas, she thought with a sigh, was too much on her mind lately.

She climbed down into the dig from the lowest point, her interest fixed on the heap of tumbled earth and rocks that covered the spot she knew the sculpture to be, and her heart was thudding hard at her ribs as she contemplated it. Down on her knees a few moments later she carefully scraped away the dry soil and peered closely for a first sight of her prize.

A smooth rounded glimpse of marble renewed her optimism and her energy, for it stood out in contrast to the rougher red rocks that buried it, and she began again, scraping with her trowel and scarcely daring to breathe as she restrained her impatience. She was completely engrossed and unaware of anything, until a voice called down from the rim of the hollow and she jerked her head up swiftly.

'Bethany!'

The rest of the words were drowned in the crackling rumble of slipping earth and rocks, and a minor avalanche rolled downwards in the same moment that she was swept off her feet and bowled sideways, over and over, with a pair of strong arms wrapped tightly around her. Then for a few seconds the air was uncannily still and quiet, and red dust obscured her hazy glimpse of the sky.

She wasn't hurt; perhaps bruised a little from being rolled over on the ground, but surprise and alarm at the unexpectedness of it were not the prime cause of her wildly erratic heartbeat. It was realising that the arms wrapped so tightly and protectively around her belonged to Nikolas. The burning heat of a masculine body lay on top of her and completely smothered her

except for a minute glimpse of sky she had between his
head and one broad shoulder, and the hard fierce
thudding of his heart pulsed heavily against her breast.

He raised his head after what seemed like an eternity
and looked down at her, his face immediately above
hers so that she could see every line and angle of those
stern features and the blazing fierceness in his eyes.
The sun beating down on her face made her half-
close her eyes against its glare and she breathed fast
and unevenly through parted lips, stunningly conscious
of the muscular weight that pinned her down. Nikolas's mouth was hard, set in a straight line that betrayed his fury as surely as did the glitter in his eyes,
and Bethany felt herself shaking despite the pressure
that held her on the ground.

'You little fool!' He hissed the words between tight
lips, and they breathed hotly on her mouth. 'You dis-
obedient, stubborn little fool!'

Bethany drew a breath to say something, she was
never sure what, but before she could utter a word he
smothered her mouth with his and all the suppressed
fury in his voice was given rein in the violence of his
kiss. She tried to move, making a small unintelligible
sound of protest, but it never quite formed, and she
succumbed breathlessly to a kind of excitement she
had never known existed, while Nikolas bore down on
her more fiercely, almost as if he sought to force her
into the hard stony ground.

'Niko!'

Her response was an almost unrecognisable whisper
when he freed her mouth, and her lips brushed the hot
smooth skin of his jaw while he buried his face in the
curve of her shoulder. It seemed that her body no
longer belonged to her, and she had never felt so wildly
exultant as she did at that moment. Her head turned
back and forth while his mouth moved slowly over her
neck and throat, hot and bruisingly hard, upwards to
her mouth once more. But when she twisted under
him, freeing her arms and putting them around his

neck, it was as if the movement brought him to realisation.

'Niko?'

She looked into his face, seeing the passion that burned in his dark eyes and the sensual thrust of his mouth as he gazed down at her. But while she watched through drooping lashes, his expression began to show a subtle change, and he was looking at her as if she was a stranger suddenly, a small frown suggesting that he found something unexpected in her response.

Then he let her go, slowly and with apparent reluctance, his hands sliding from around her in a curiously caressing movement. 'Are you hurt?'

The question had a strangely flat sound after the elation of the past few minutes, and Bethany recalled hazily that he had asked much the same question the last time he kissed her. She shook her head without speaking, and after a second or two he got to his feet, leaving her there on the stony ground, watching him cautiously and trying to bring herself back to earth.

He brushed the red dust from his clothes with sharp, hard gestures and he didn't look at her, then, as if he suddenly realised, he reached for her hands and raised her to her feet, retaining his hold on her for a moment but still not looking directly at her. 'Are you quite sure you're unhurt?'

'Yes, yes I'm quite sure, Niko.' Her voice sounded strangely husky still and she brushed down her dress with hands that she just had to keep busy because they were shaking so much. Then she laughed lightly in a not very successful attempt at levity that was meant to bring the situation strictly into perspective. 'Lucky you came after me!'

'I'm glad you find it amusing!' He was no longer avoiding her eyes as he had in the first few seconds after they got to their feet, and she saw that the heat of anger now burned where passion had been before. 'You deliberately disobeyed me!' he said harshly. 'It was because I'm beginning to know your penchant for stubbornness and your dislike of not getting your own way that I followed you! If I hadn't you would probably be lying there under that last earth-fall, and I'm in no mind to give you as a human sacrifice to your precious god, whatever you believe!'

'Nikolas, I only——'

'Don't make excuses!' Nikolas ordered sharply. 'You can't deny that you completely ignored my warning about possible danger simply because you had to have your own way. Holy Mother, do you imagine I say these things merely for the pleasure of hearing my own voice, child?'

'*Child?*' Again she picked on the word that of all the things he ever called her pricked her the most, and she turned on him swiftly, her eyes bright with defiance. Her courage inspired by the memory of the same mouth that now looked so tightly angry. 'You didn't treat me much like a child a few minutes ago,' she charged huskily. 'And considering the lengths I've known you to go to preserve my reputation, you were taking quite a chance! Or was that all part of my training?'

She was speaking rashly and unfairly, she realised it the moment she saw his expression, but at the moment his strict ruling regarding his brother's behaviour towards her did not make much sense. She had never seen him look so furiously angry and she took an instinctive step backwards away from him, her eyes wide and suddenly wary.

'If you——'

His mouth twisted into the harsh mockery of a smile, and he thrust both hands into the pockets of his slacks. 'Obviously you realise what you deserve,' he said. 'God knows why I'm so lenient with you, but this is the very last time, my girl, you'd better remember that! From now on you do exactly as you're told, do you understand?' Bethany was too choked to say anything, but she looked up at him with mingled anger and frustration showing in her eyes, and gave a barely perceptible nod. 'Good!' Nikolas said shortly. 'If I catch you here again I shall make you sorry you were ever born, believe me!'

'Nikolas!' She made the protest when he encircled

her wrist with his long fingers and took her with him
across the dusty hollow. 'The Apollo, I——'

'The Apollo will stay where it is until someone with
more skill and authority comes to recover it,' Nikolas
told her adamantly.

Again Bethany tried to appeal to him, but he had a
firm, hard look about him that told her she would be
wasting her time, so she cast a last glance in the direction of the even bigger pile of rubble covering the
Apollo, and shrugged. She allowed herself to be helped
out on to the hillside again, and followed with apparent meekness when he led the way back to the
house.

Let him think he had things his own way; there
would be other times, other opportunities. She just
wished it was easier to forget the crushing weight of his
body and the burning excitement of his mouth; and it
made her distinctly uneasy to realise that she enjoyed
provoking Nikolas in a way she would never have
dreamed of doing with any other man.

More restless than ever and uneasily defensive in Nikolas's company, Bethany was distracted only a couple
of days later by the arrival of two men who came via
the island ferry. In shorts and denim shirts they arrived carrying an assortment of paraphernalia in rucksacks and were met on the quay by Nikolas. The
information was conveyed to her by Takis who had
apparently seen them come, and the moment she
heard about them Bethany was avid for more information; new arrivals were rare in Apolidus and of interest
to everyone on the island.

'Who were they, Takis, do you have any ideas?' she
asked.

It was Takis's way these days to assume an air of
nonchalance, as if island affairs no longer interested
him and he waited only for the day when he could
leave Apolidus and take up his new and more exciting
life. He was getting ready to go and join some of the
village boys in a game of football when he told Beth-

any about the new arrivals, and he was not very interested, so he merely shrugged.

'Business perhaps?' he suggested, but Bethany shook her head.

'Not if they were dressed in shorts and carrying rucksacks,' she decided with certainty. 'They sound more like——' An idea struck her suddenly and she frowned at Takis curiously. 'They sound more like archaeologists, don't they?'

'They could be,' Takis agreed obligingly.

Bethany was juggling with the idea of risking Nikolas's wrath and leaving her kitchen chores to go and see for herself. 'Did you notice where they went?' she asked Takis, and he shrugged, obviously neither knowing nor caring, so that she felt a twitch of impatience.

'I don't know—into the *taverna* maybe?'

'Not with Nikolas!' She knew she was safe to assume that Nikolas would never have taken businessmen to the *taverna*, any more than businessmen were likely to be wearing shorts and carrying packs. 'Takis, are you sure they didn't go up the hill, towards the dig?'

Just for a moment it seemed she had his interest, and he eyed her curiously. 'The dig?' He pursed his lower lip in imitation of Nikolas, then pulled a face. 'Maybe,' he agreed. 'I suppose they could have, I didn't really notice.' He eyed her steadily for a moment and it occurred to her in that moment that Takis was rapidly changing from the little brother she had always known into a youth approaching thirteen. It seemed for a moment almost as if he was rapidly catching up with her and closing that five-and-a-half-year gap between them. 'Why?' he demanded, again in imitation of Nikolas. 'What makes you think they've gone to the dig, Beth?'

In as few words as possible, she told him of Nikolas's promise to have their discovery unearthed by someone more qualified, and she realised as she told him, just how detached from one another their lives had become lately. At one time she would not have needed to tell him anything about their dig, he would have been as well informed as she was herself, and as interested. Could he, she wondered, recall the man on the quay?

'Oh well——' He shrugged, making it obvious that his interest had been only passing. 'Maybe Nikolas has taken them to the site and they'll get the Apollo for you.'

'And for *you*,' said Bethany, unable to resist the reminder that he had been one of the original finders. 'Takis, do you remember if the man you spoke to on the quay that evening looked anything like the Apollo?'

He wrinkled his brow for a moment, but it was clear that he had little or no recollection of the man. 'I can't honestly say I remember what he looked like,' he confessed after a second or two, 'but it was almost dark, Beth, and I didn't really take a lot of notice of him.'

It had been a possibility all along, Bethany recognised, but she doubted very much if Nikolas was going to give much credence to her story without Takis's support, and she sighed deeply as she turned back in to the kitchen. 'Then there's only my word for it, and Nikolas isn't going to believe that. Not that it really matters whether he does or not,' she added after consideration. 'It doesn't make any difference if I know I'm right.'

In fact Nikolas was unexpectedly forthcoming when he returned to the house, and when she brought him his coffee outside on the terrace, he asked her to sit down, he had something to tell her. The two men, he explained, had insisted on lunching at the *taverna* and had returned on the afternoon ferry to Siros. Time was short and the Apollo had been easier to recover than Nikolas had anticipated.

'Then it *is* Apollo?' said Bethany, her eyes gleaming with anticipation, and Nikolas hesitated before he answered.

'It seems likely that it's some kind of Apollo,' he allowed, and she fidgeted with impatience because he was being so cautious.

In the shade of the plane tree that overhung the table his face had that hint of the Orient about it, as the shifting dark shadows emphasised the contours of cheekbones and eyes. She had not realised before how much more often she watched his face lately; fascinated by the austere strength of the features and the mouth that looked so stern but could soften almost uncannily when he smiled, or kiss so fiercely that it took her breath away.

'What exactly does that mean?' she asked curiously. 'Some kind of Apollo?'

'It means,' Nikolas told her with pedantic precision, 'that there's a possibility the sculpture isn't very old after all.' He saw the way her face fell, and held up a cautionary hand. 'Don't be too discouraged yet,' he advised. 'The two men who came this morning are on the staff of someone I've known for some years now, and they're almost certain, but the Professor has the last word, of course.'

Bethany sat at the table facing him and with her hands supporting her chin, her eyes fixed anxiously on his face. 'The Professor?'

'His name is Professor Carl Bailey, and you can rely on his opinion, Bethany.'

He sipped his coffee, then reached for a piece of the *loukoumi* he showed such an unexpected partiality for, and Bethany wished he was not so intent on taking his time, for he had something else in store for her yet, she felt sure. He licked the powdery white sugar with obvious pleasure before putting the rose-flavoured jelly into his mouth, and his eyes were hidden from her while he concentrated on what he was doing instead of looking across at her.

'Nikolas?' she prompted him anxiously, and he licked his lips with the tip of his tongue in a curiously sensual gesture of pleasure.

'I shall take you to Siros tomorrow,' he told her, making no pretence of consulting her wishes in the matter. 'Takis will be in school and Aunt Alexia has, I believe, some arrangement with one of the village women concerning a sick child, so we shall go alone.'

Her heart was thudding, but somehow she managed to control her voice. 'To Siros?' He nodded, taking another morsel of *loukoumi* from the dish. 'To see your friend Professor Bailey?'

'It was through him that I was able to arrange the excavation of your Apollo so quickly,' Nikolas explained, licking sugar from his fingers, and for the first time Bethany realised just how much effort he had taken to get the Apollo recovered for her. 'By tomorrow,' he went on, 'he'll have had time to decide whether or not you've made a real find, or——' He used his hands to express what he obviously believed to be the more likely, and Bethany tried quickly to bring her wandering thoughts to some kind of order.

'You mean—it's gone? They've taken it away?'

For a moment his brows gathered into the more familiar frown, and his tone hinted at impatience. 'You'll see it again tomorrow, child, don't make so much fuss!' Briefly she met his eyes and found them fixed on her unwaveringly so that she hastily averted her own gaze from him again. 'You weren't thinking of turning down the trip to Siros, were you, Bethany?'

'No, of course not! It's just that I'm rather surprised at you taking me——' She bit back the words hastily, for the last thing she wanted to do was make him angry, just when things were going her way. 'I'm sure your professor friend will confirm that the Apollo *is* ancient,' she told him. 'And I'm anxious to see it again to—to convince myself how much like it the other Apollo is.'

'You know, of course, that Takis was unable to remember him well enough to confirm your rather extravagant claims for him?'

Her colour rose, but Bethany held firmly on to her temper, for she couldn't afford to annoy him now. 'It isn't extravagant, Nikolas,' she insisted, 'but I don't expect you to take my word for it. I've already accepted that it's something I simply can't prove, but *I* know he's Apollo.'

When she looked at him again it startled her to realise how much more gentle his mood was, and his stern mouth was smiling slightly. He reached across the table and stroked a long forefinger down her cheek and it was as much as she could do not to close her eyes in sheer ecstasy. Although realising just how much he could affect her brought on that now familiar and disturbing uneasiness she felt so often in his company lately.

'You dream too much, little one,' he murmured softly, 'and sometimes I fear for you when you have to leave this safe little paradise of yours and join the rest of us in the outside world. You have such—promise, but I shall have to guide you very slowly and carefully so as not to wake you too soon to what life is all about.'

But even while her blood ran fast at the touch of his hand and the softness of his voice, she felt a moment of panic at the idea of being hauled forcibly from her beloved island, and she leaned back from the caressing hand and shook her head. There was reproach and wariness in her eyes and a soft vulnerability about her mouth as she looked across at him, because she couldn't forget the plans he had for her and Theo.

'Is taking me to Siros with you just part of preparing me for being dragged into your more practical world, Nikolas?' she asked huskily, and his eyes narrowed just a fraction, she noticed.

'It's the only way you're going to see your Apollo again,' he told her. 'Whether or not you come with me is entirely up to you, Bethany!'

Of course Bethany went. How could she do anything other than go? The trip was nothing like as long as the journey to Rhodes had been, but they travelled by the same method, and it seemed like no time at all before Nikolas was nosing the motor cruiser into the harbour at Ermoupolis, once the biggest port in Greece. She had time to recognise the twin hills amid the modern waterfront, each one topped by a huge cathedral and dominating the ancient city once dedicated to the god Hermes.

From the harbour they took a taxi to the outskirts of the city where Nikolas's professor friend had his home, and she had a little time to admire the handsome public buildings that surrounded a central square, raised like a dais and supporting a bandstand. Seeing her interest Nikolas smiled, and looked at her in such a way that she suddenly flushed warmly and quickly looked out of the taxi window again.

The house they sought was Greek in design, but furnished with such Englishness that Bethany realised she was getting her first glimpse of what an English home looked like, and she found it strangely foreign. It was comfortable but somewhat shabby, and the furniture suggested that it might have come out with the Professor when he first came to Greece nearly forty years before.

'Miss Meandis, welcome.' He greeted her in the Greek fashion but in English, and Bethany was surprised to hear Nikolas speaking English with a pronounced and very attractive accent. It was the first time she had any inkling that he even spoke it at all. 'Please forgive me,' the Professor went on as he saw them seated and offered the traditional hospitality. 'Although I have lived in your lovely country for so many years, I've never acquired the ability to converse easily in your language.' He gave Nikolas a grateful nod and smiled. 'My Greek friends are kind enough to indulge me, and put me to shame by speaking excellent English.'

It was on the tip of Bethany's tongue to tell him that she wasn't in fact Greek, but a fellow countrywoman of his, but that would have delayed the matter they had come to discuss. Professor Bailey was one of the foremost authorities on Greek antiquities, so Nikolas had told her, and he was very obviously deeply involved with his subject.

Also the bust of Apollo stood on a small table between them and from the moment she came into the room she had been unable to take her eyes from it. The features were, she was more convinced that ever, exactly like those of the man who had called himself Apollo, and to her it was nothing short of a miracle. She longed to tell the Professor about it, but first he must give them his opinion on its authenticity.

'You're anxious to hear about your friend here, of course,' he said indicating the bust, and he smiled at Bethany's obvious eagerness. 'I'm afraid I have a disappointment for you, my dear Miss Meandis.' Bethany's heart sank as he picked up the Apollo from the table and balanced it on his knee, grimacing at the weight of it. 'This handsome fellow is definitely not two thousand years old, nor even two hundred; in fact I can date him almost exactly. He was worked about twenty years ago by a very talented young compatriot of mine, who is alas no longer alive.' He smoothed a hand over the two wings of hair held back by the traditional fillet bound round the noble brow. 'Her name was Megan Scott, and it was always my desire to meet her, for she produced work that the ancients would have been proud of. This is a very good example of what she could do, and in fact I happen to have heard about this particular piece.'

Bethany was trying to cope with the realisation that the sculpted head that had caused her so much unrest in the past weeks was actually her mother's work. She had never been allowed into her mother's studio, although Pavlos had never made such a ruling concerning his own domain, and she had never really known just how skilled her mother was until this moment.

She did not look at Nikolas for the moment, but at the Professor's thoughtful face as he studied the Apollo he held on his knee, and she licked her lips nervously before she ventured further. 'It—it is meant to be Apollo, isn't it?' she asked, and Professor Bailey smiled.

'Oh yes, most certainly it is, my dear young lady, but not the traditional god we're more used to seeing. You see how the hair differs for one thing; it's straight instead of the more usual curls, and the curious flyaway effect of the wings of hair above the forehead.'

He followed the skilfully sculpted lines with his finger, and Bethany followed its trace as if mesmerised by it. 'Oh yes, it *is* an Apollo, but not the god, only a very down-to-earth and, unless I've been misled by gossip, a rather unreliable man. His name was Apollo, although I believe he also had a less exotic name as well which I can't remember at the moment. He was an Anglo-Greek and the story goes that Megan Scott was quite besotted with him, so much so that she made him in the image of his more exalted namesake because she wanted to please him. He was her husband, after all, so I suppose it was natural—Apollo Scott, a rather fanciful combination, you must allow.'

Bethany's head jerked round almost of its own volition and she stared at Nikolas unbelievingly, catching for a moment a look of shock that told how stunned he was by the outcome. Her hands were tightly clasped, but she hoped that her obvious agitation would be attributed to simple disappointment.

'He's—he's very handsome,' she murmured, without really knowing what she said.

All she could think of was that the man who had sat beside her, even talked to her, on the hillside that evening had been her father and he had not even given her a clue to his identity. There was a chilling numbness in her that clutched at her stomach muscles until she felt physically sick when she faced the fact that he had deliberately kept the information from her, even after he knew who she was. Nikolas would surely not doubt her word now that the two Apollos, marble and flesh and blood, had been proved to be images of one another.

Still trying to keep up the pretence of being uninvolved, she avoided looking at Nikolas now, for the pity and compassion in his eyes had almost proved her undoing. Instead she kept her eyes on the tauntingly handsome features that had haunted her for so long. Perhaps it had not simply been because of her mother's sculpture of him that he had seemed so familiar, but because she recalled him from somewhere in her deliberately forgotten childhood. Before Papa adopted her and taught her what it was like to be loved.

'Handsome is as handsome does, as the saying goes, eh?' Professor Bailey suggested, and placed the marble back on to the table where it seemed to gaze at them down its arrogantly handsome nose. 'This fellow wasn't a god by all accounts, although maybe he found those godlike looks pretty hard to live with.' He looked across at Nikolas, and Bethany was given a brief respite in which to gather her shattered wits together. 'I'm sorry to disappoint you, my dear fellow,' he told Nikolas, 'but even though it isn't an antiquity, it has some value as Megan Scott's work. She did so little before she was killed, poor girl, so it has a rarity value; although heaven knows how this beautiful piece came to be buried on your little island.'

Bethany had a feeling that she knew, but this was not the moment to say so; she would tell Nikolas later and have little doubt that he would believe what she said now. While the two men talked, she managed to bring herself under control, and it crossed her mind as she listened to them that Nikolas was making conversation with just that in mind. He glanced at her every so often, but made no attempt to draw her into the conversation, speaking in his slow and attractively pedantic English about matters she could hardly be expected to follow.

Nikolas declined an invitation to lunch on behalf of them both, saying that they had made other arrangements. In fact Bethany was relieved to find it wasn't true, for she did not in the least feel like sitting in a public place and eating a meal as if nothing had happened. She had never felt a more urgent need to fly back to Apolidus and the familiar surroundings.

It was a little surprising too how thankfully she reverted to Greek the moment they left their host, and Nikolas's light hand on her arm as they went in search of a taxi brought a lump to her throat that she fought hard to swallow without bringing tears to her eyes. She shook her head when he offered her lunch, and he

did not insist, but had the taxi take them directly to
the waterfront; a drive that was made in almost complete silence.

It was not until they were once more skimming
smoothly across the blue silken surface of the Aegean
that the question of the Apollos was mentioned. As
he turned to look at her, Nikolas's eyes had a deep dark
warmth that was almost like an embrace, and seemed
to recognise how close to tears she was. She stood beside
him at the wheel of the cruiser instead of seeking the
solitariness of the small cabin, because there was an un-
believable comfort in his nearness, and the sight of
his tall, lean figure, feet planted firmly apart, was more
reassuring than anything.

'I'm sorry, Bethany.' The words were muffled in part
by the hum of the engine, but she knew how much he
regretted the outcome of their trip, and she shook her
head.

'You couldn't know,' she whispered soundlessly, and
he stretched out an arm suddenly and pulled her close
to his side, resting his chin on the bright tawny softness of her hair, his arm firm and comforting about her
waist. 'I don't blame you, Nikolas, it's just that——'
She choked on the admission as if she was ashamed of
it. 'I liked him; I actually liked him, and he——'

'Sssh! Of course you liked him, you silly child, it
wouldn't be natural if you didn't, but you mustn't
dwell on it too much and make yourself miserable over
what is, after all, no new situation, is it?'

His arm tightened and the broad hand below her
breast stroked soothingly as he hugged her closer for
a moment and kissed her forehead. Drawing courage
from it, she poured out the bitterness she felt at being
brushed aside for a second time by her natural father,
and Nikolas let her talk, simply holding her close
while they streaked across the water leaving a trail of
feathery foam in their wake. She cried a little, but for
the most part there was too much anger in her to feel
sorry for herself.

'How could he have sat there and—and talked to me

as he did, without saying something?' she asked, for the hundreth time. 'He even told me he had no taste for a home and family, but he didn't tell me that he'd once had a family and deserted them!'

'Your mother went back to him, Bethany.' She jerked her head round swiftly to look up into his face, her eyelids blinking rapidly because she knew it was true and that she didn't want to have it confirmed. 'I came to Apolidus that first time, do you remember?' Nikolas went on, and she nodded. How could she forget that first time? She had felt so sure he despised her then that she had hated him for the next four years, quite unreasonably. 'Pavlos didn't talk much about her,' he said, 'but he did tell me that. I think it was the hardest thing he had to bear; when she left him, and yet I think, in time, he came to look upon it as just punishment for his own shortcomings in that direction.'

'I didn't know.' She slipped an arm about him and found the warm strength of him incredibly reassuring. 'But—I remember the day she went away; that night, I couldn't sleep and I heard Papa go out. I'd heard him——' She swallowed hard on the recollection of the deep, painful sobs of a grown man crying like a child in the darkness. 'I think he—— Papa took the head of Apollo and threw it into that hollow in the hillside, Niko. I think he did it that night, the night after she went back to my father.' She looked up at him again, seeking support for her theory, and Nikolas nodded slowly. 'Don't you think that's how it got there, Niko?'

'It's an unanswerable puzzle otherwise,' he replied.

'And to think— *that man* came back after all this time! And was too cowardly to tell me who he was because he was ashamed of himself!'

'That's probably more true than you realise,' Nikolas told her quietly, and once more she looked up at him.

The wind blew his hair back from a broad brow and his eyes were narrowed against the wind and the

dazzle of the sun on the water, his mouth firm but
gentle at the moment. Above all he was strong, and
that mattered very much to Bethany at the moment.
Nikolas would never walk out on his family responsibilities; that was really why he was there with her now,
because he had taken over his cousin's family and
made himself responsible for them. And yet—something struck her suddenly that had gone unnoticed
when he first spoke.

'You—you actually sound as if you're sorry for him!'
she accused, and Nikolas smiled in that curiously sardonic way he had sometimes.

'I think he might well have been too ashamed to tell
you who he really was,' he said, 'and if that's so, then I
do perhaps feel a little sorry for him. He's lost so much
and it must be very hard for a man to admit that he's
thrown away something that he realises too late is very
precious to him.'

'You—you think that's how he felt?'

She recalled the strange sound he had made in his
throat when she spoke so disparagingly of her natural
father, and the bitterness of his smile when she asked
his name and he told her Apollo. If only she had
known!

'I think it's how Pavlos felt,' Nikolas was saying
quietly, and she brought herself swiftly back to realisation. Never could she have put Papa and her natural
father into the same category, and yet Nikolas had just
done so quite logically. He caught her eye and held
her wavering and unwilling gaze determinedly, clasping her close to his side while he forced her to accept
the comparison. 'They had a great deal in common,
Bethany.'

She said nothing, feeling yet another piece of her
little world turned upside down. Heracles and his
brother must have felt very much as she felt, when they
were children, yet Heracles could remember his father
fondly and take his illegitimate brother to his heart
and into his home.

'I suppose they had,' she allowed huskily, and Nikolas bent his head to kiss her, lightly and gently on her mouth. Apolidus was already in sight and getting closer every moment, and between them Nikolas and her island could do a lot to help make her forget the betrayal of Apollo the second time around.

# CHAPTER SEVEN

BETHANY was not exactly sure what her reaction was when they returned to the house and found that Theo had put in an appearance; looking very pleased with himself, she thought, until she noticed a wary look in his eyes when he greeted his brother. Nikolas, of course, made no bones about his own opinion of the visit, and Bethany was a little puzzled by his lack of warmth; for she firmly believed he was fond of Theo, even if he did occasionally wield the stick of authority over him.

'How the devil did you get here?' he demanded.

'I took the ferry to Piraeus and then took a local ferry here,' Theo told him, and was quite evidently pleased with his ingenuity in finding his way around without the accustomed convenience of private transport. ' I arrived about half an hour ago.'

'And for what purpose?' Nikolas asked with crushing practicality. Alexia was serving Theo with coffee and displaying the same kind of doting adoration shown by his mother; an attitude that Nikolas viewed with a hint of exasperation. 'Presumably you had a reason for coming,' he went on, 'or you wouldn't have gone to so much trouble and discomfort. Public transport isn't quite your style, is it, Theo?'

Bethany sat at the other end of the table, taking a so far silent interest in what was going on. She had far too much on her mind at the moment to give Theo the welcome he very obviously expected, but he seemed undeterred by her present reticence, confident of his welcome.

'I wanted to see Bethany again,' he told Nikolas, and beamed her a smile as he said it. She was appalled to realise that she was blushing and more still to realise that Aunt Alexia very obviously approved of his reasons, if not his actions. Theo caught her eye and winked, much too confident to be defeated by anything less than a direct snub. 'You *are* glad to see me, aren't you, Beth?'

His use of the abbreviation of her name that until now had been Takis's prerogative added to her confusion, and she glanced instinctively at Nikolas when her hand was seized and her fingers lightly kissed. She noted the tight line of his mouth with genuine regret and knew she would find it hard to forgive Theo if his coming upset the new and rather exciting rapport she had with Nikolas, forgetting his plans to marry her to Theo.

'Of course I'm glad to see you, Theo,' she said, taking care not to make it sound too much as if there was anything intimate in her welcome. 'I think you'll like Apolidus.'

In fact she doubted very much if he would enjoy her precious island for very long, for Theo was not made for the quiet life, but it was unthinkable to admit, even to herself, that she simply had no idea what to say to him. Theo always gave her the uneasy feeling that deep inside he might find her unworldliness rather amusing and it inhibited her to some extent where he was concerned.

Nikolas, however, was far less reticent about saying exactly what he thought, and he eyed his younger brother with a hint of mockery in his eyes. 'I estimate it will take you less than twenty-four hours to become utterly bored with what Apolidus has to offer in the way of amusement,' he told him, and gave Bethany a brief smile, as if to assure her that it was not his own opinion, only one he attributed to his brother. 'No restaurants, no roads,' he went on, 'no theatres and no clubs, only the *taverna* and the talk of the farmers and fishermen. I guarantee you'll be bored within a few hours, Theo.'

'Are *you*?' Theo challenged, and Bethany did not realise just how anxiously she watched for Nikolas's response.

Nikolas sipped his coffee slowly, but there was an air of restrained tension about him and she noticed how white his knuckles were as he clasped the tiny cup. 'No,' he said quietly, 'but I don't demand quite so much out of each day as you do, brother.'

It was clear that Theo did not like the trend of the conversation, and he always seemed at a slight disadvantage whenever he tried crossing swords with Nikolas, Bethany had noticed it before. Theo knew it and he resented it; it showed in the short, harsh bark of laughter as he shook his head. 'Oh, but of course you don't have any option but to stay here, do you? You have to stay and keep watch on your flock, and particularly on your ewe lamb, to see that the wolves don't ravish her!'

'Theodore!'

He fell silent at once, the mocking laughter dying uneasily, for it had been an act of bravado, no more, and he was sorry for it, it was obvious. He heaved his shoulders in regret, avoiding Alexia's reproachful eyes. 'I'm sorry, Niko.'

To Bethany it was incredible the way he backed down before Nikolas's disapproval, and she wondered that she could ever have thought herself capable of defying him and getting away with it, when someone as bold and confident as Theo eventually yielded. It possibly had to do with the fact that Nikolas had been *in locum parentis* for his own father for far longer than he had for Papa. Also he was a good deal older than both Theo and herself and therefore commanded a certain respect, even from a liberal thinker like Theo.

Nikolas did not pursue the question of why he was there, but brought them back to more practical matters with his usual expediency. 'Have you taken yourself a room at the *taverna*?' he asked, and must surely have known the sensation he was going to cause before he spoke.

Theo gazed at him blankly for a moment, then switched his unbelieving gaze to Alexia, who looked equally stunned. 'The *taverna*?' His gaze travelled along the walls of the sprawling old house, half sub-merged in its jungle of shrubs and looking deceptively large. 'I thought——' he began, but Nikolas was shak-ing his head.

'The house is too small to accommodate even an-other one,' he told Theo. 'You'll have to see what the *taverna* has to offer; I believe they take the occasional visitor if needs be.'

There was the studio, Bethany thought, but he did not mention that. Of course it wasn't equipped to sleep anyone, let alone a young man accustomed to the luxuries of life, but as a makeshift measure it would surely have served well enough. Theo, it was clear, still did not quite believe he was being refused the hos-pitality he felt entitled to, and he looked at Nikolas with narrowed eyes.

'You expect me to stay at the *taverna*?'

'I see no alternative,' Nikolas informed him coolly. 'As you said, I have to guard my ewe lamb from the wolves, and frankly, my dear brother, I shall feel con-siderably easier in my mind if you're sleeping at the *taverna* and not under this roof.' He sounded so coolly logical about it all that Bethany scarcely believed the implications he was making, and she gazed at him wide-eyed as he got to his feet and stood toweringly tall over his brother. 'If you prefer,' Nikolas went on, smoothly practical, 'I can go and see Petrakis and see what can be done about finding you a room. How long will you be needing it for?'

'Damn it, *I* don't know!' Theo fumed in exaspera-tion. 'I didn't expect to be treated as if I've brought the plague with me!'

Nikolas stood for a moment or two, considering, then he nodded as if he had worked it out to his satis-faction. 'On second thoughts, I'll give you forty-eight hours instead of twenty-four for the charms of Apolidus to pall,' he told his brother. 'If you need it for longer——' He shrugged as if he doubted that was very likely, then went striding off, presumably to ar-range the necessary accommodation.

'A fine welcome!' Theo complained as he watched

his brother depart, although he must have been sure that one person at least welcomed his unexpected arrival. 'Don't you think I deserve better treatment from my brother, Aunt Alex?'

Such an appeal could not fail, and Alexia looked at him with mingled reproach and resignation. 'Oh, but of course you're welcome, Theo,' she assured him. 'But you should take more care not to annoy Niko by speaking to him so—rashly about matters he takes very seriously. As guardian to Takis and Bethany, Niko feels his responsibilities deeply, and does his best to protect their interests. You should remember that.'

Such gentle scoldings as Alexia gave him did not trouble Theo in the least, he could shrug them off easily. What apparently concerned him at the moment was Bethany's so far rather lukewarm reception of him, and he determined to do something about it. Reaching for her hand, he held it tightly, kissing her fingers with a mere brush of his lips. '*You're* glad to see me, aren't you, Bethany?' he pleaded.

'That's something else, Theo,' Alexia told him. 'You shouldn't be so—bold in your approach to Bethany. You know how Nikolas dislikes any display of——'

'Independence?' Theo suggested, and his voice betrayed the impatience he felt for such caution. 'Sweet Aunt Alex, such restrictions are going out of fashion and you must surely realise it. One no longer has to sit and simply look at a young woman when she is beautiful, it is not considered necessary to treat a lovely girl as if she was too sacred to be—touched.' He traced a finger along Bethany's arm, and smiled.

A faint flush coloured Alexia's wrinkled brown cheeks. 'Perhaps,' she conceded cautiously, 'but I cannot help regretting the passing of some of our old customs, just as Nikolas does.'

'Dear sweet aunt,' Theo drawled, and kissed her cheek with obviously genuine affection. 'Niko is a tyrant and you know it. He keeps a hard hand on Bethany and the other women in his family, but takes his pleasure where the women are less strictly controlled. I call that having double standards!'

'Theo!' Very obviously Alexia did not like the
trend of the conversation at all, but she could not have
thought herself capable of stopping it if Theo was of
a mind to continue. 'Foreign women are different, and
they——'

'Not only foreign women,' Theo argued. 'Greek
women too, Aunt Alex; they're not all under the
thumb of men like him, you know.'

Alexia's softly gentle face was flushed, and if anger
had ever showed in her eyes it did at that moment, for
she had a very genuine respect as well as love for his
older brother. 'Theo, I cannot allow that!' she insisted in a voice more forceful than any Bethany had
ever heard her use. 'You speak as if Niko was the most
unprincipled rake, and I refuse to believe you're not
exaggerating out of all proportion!'

Bethany had been listening with a curious kind of
shrinking feeling inside her, and she as well as Alexia
looked at Theo, waiting for him to confess to being
wrong, or at least to exaggerating. It was a moment
before he did anything at all, and then he beamed his
dazzling smile at his aunt and kissed her again, loudly
and enthusiastically, charming his way back into her
good graces.

'Of course I exaggerate, dear aunt,' he told her, 'but I
cannot allow you to be deluded into believing Nikolas
is as strictly puritanical as he might appear. He has a
fondness for beautiful women that is at least equal to
mine, although of course *his* tastes run more towards
the sophisticated older woman. He's a man with the
same desires as the rest of us, and he's never allowed his
views to restrict him to my knowledge!'

Bethany was feeling very small and inexplicably
chill, and the protest she made was purely instinctive,
because she could remember too clearly how it felt to
be in Nikolas's arms, and the burning fierceness of his
kisses. 'Don't talk like that, Theo!'

'Bethany?'

They both turned their heads and were looking at

her as if they suspected she had suddenly taken leave of
her senses, and it was during the ensuing few seconds
that she realised just how vehement she had been.
Swallowing hard, she made an effort to counter the impression, shaking her head as she sought the right
words to explain her outburst.

'It—it just doesn't seem right to talk about Nikolas
like that when he isn't here,' she explained, and Theo's
arched brow was faintly sardonic.

Obviously he was taken aback, but his kind of confidence was quickly recovered and he was smiling
again. 'I wouldn't dare speak about him like that when
he *is* here,' he admitted with disarming candour. But
her objection had obviously puzzled him and he
sought a reason for it other than the one she offered.
Taking her hand, he twined her slender fingers with
his. 'I'm surprised to hear you objecting, Bethany.'

She preferred not to meet his eyes, and experienced
a curious sense of shyness suddenly with those faintly
quizzical dark eyes watching her. 'I just don't think it's
right to talk about anyone on that subject when he's
not here to give lie to what you say.'

'Give lie?' Theo enquired gently, and brushed his
lips across her fingers while he continued to watch her.

'He *is* your brother,' Bethany reminded him.

'Exactly,' Theo agreed in a quiet and unexpectedly
sober voice, 'and in the circumstances I can claim to
know him pretty well. But not as well, it seems, as you
do, pretty cousin.'

Bethany gave a brief, appealing glance in Alexia's
direction, but Alexia seemed to be as puzzled by her
attitude as Theo was. 'I didn't say I knew him well,' she
denied, but Theo was smiling as if something about
the situation intrigued him.

'Who knows better how—traditional he can be?' he
said. 'You must have hated having your wings clipped
after the freedom you had enjoyed while Pavlos was
alive. You must have hated *him*, eh?'

Alexia was looking at her very oddly and Bethany
wished she had not been so impulsively fervent about

her objection. 'Of course I don't—I didn't hate him,' she denied. 'That's much too—too melodramatic, Theo!'

She recalled telling Alexia just how much she hated Nikolas the very first day he arrived there, but that seemed so long ago now, and a lot of things had changed. Not least her feelings towards Nikolas, although she did not stop to decide what exactly they were at that moment. Her whole emotional situation was in far too much doubt to be put into words. Instead she tried to explain that she was much less resentful than she had once been.

'I haven't found it too bad,' she told him, 'although I admit that I resented being scolded and disciplined so often at first, until I realised it was quite reasonable to expect me to help Aunt Alex. Now——'

'Now?' Theo prompted softly, and she passed the tip of her tongue anxiously over her lips, remembering how thankful she had been for Nikolas's strength and comfort only a couple of hours since.

'Now I'm used to him,' she confessed. 'He has a lot of good points and most of the things he says make sense, and he can be very—gentle.'

'*Aie!*' Theo murmured softly, and his dark, bright eyes watched the colour warm her cheeks. 'What has he done to bring about such a conversion, eh?'

'Theo.'

Once more Alexia's gentle voice warned him, but it was fairly clear that Bethany's reply troubled her in some way from the way she was looking at her and frowning slightly. Theo turned and smiled at her, but yet again quickly reverted his eyes to Bethany. 'I won't press the point,' he promised, having apparently taken heed of his aunt's warning after all, 'but take care, little cousin. That's far too fierce a lion for *you* to tame, and you could get hurt.'

'You're talking nonsense, Theo!' She refused to take the implication seriously, especially in view of Nikolas's plans for her concerning Theo. 'You of all people should know how he plans to marry me off!'

The fact of Nikolas's preparing her for marriage with his brother rose once more to trouble her, and she almost wished she could have felt more deeply about Theo. All she felt was a liking, an affection even, but nothing like love, as she had always thought of it, and she could only cling to Nikolas's promise that he would never make her marry someone she did not love.

But Theo was frowning at her curiously. 'Me?' he asked, and he looked so genuinely puzzled that she could not doubt he knew nothing about the combined future Nikolas had planned for them.

She shook her head uneasily, realising that Alexia looked so anxious because she had passed on something that Nikolas had told her in confidence, and she did her best to cover her near slip. 'Well, you're surely in his confidence, aren't you?' she asked, and realised that she sounded just a little too bright and breathless. 'I thought he might have told you who my bridegroom was to be.'

'Not a word,' Theo assured her, but she noticed that he was much more sober suddenly, and watched her closely while he spoke. 'But you won't let him get away with that, surely, Bethany? Not with marrying you off to somebody you might not even like.'

'Oh, I won't,' she said, but hoped it would never come to the point of having to openly defy Nikolas on that particular question. With a shrug she got up from the table and began to clear away the coffee cups, her smile strangely wistful. 'He did promise that I shouldn't have to marry anyone I don't love, and I'm sure he won't break his word; not Niko.'

'Oh, he won't,' Theo agreed quietly, and she looked across and caught his eye, noticing how darkly serious they were. 'But not being made to marry someone you *don't* love isn't quite the same as being able to marry someone you *do* love, is it, cousin?'

Bethany stood for a moment, studying his darkly handsome face and trying to follow his meaning. Then she shook her head and began once more to gather up the coffee cups. 'I imagine not,' she said.

Bethany had seldom suffered from sleeplessness, but sleep seemed impossible for her that night. Theo had gone very reluctantly to claim the room that Nikolas had booked for him at the *taverna*, and left no one in any doubt that he did not consider he was being treated as he should be. Alexia would clearly like to have offered him space in Takis's room, but she would never openly go against Nikolas's wishes.

Bethany had felt a curious sense of relief that he would not be sleeping in the house, although she could not really have said why she did not trust Theo in the same way she did his brother. Particularly in view of those discomfiting remarks he had made about Nikolas's penchant for the opposite sex. Not that she believed he was anything like as bad as Theo implied, she told herself, but there was something oddly disturbing about thinking of him with other women.

It must have been about two or three in the morning, Bethany guessed, when she got out of bed, and her restlessness was such that she went roaming quietly downstairs. There was a moon, a little past full, and she needed no other light to find her way for she knew every inch of the old house by heart. She passed through the living-room and her nightgown whispered, softly pale, past the familiar looming shapes of the furniture, and along to her stepfather's studio.

She had no idea why she had come there. But standing in the familiar room among the evidence of Pavlos's creativity she felt comfortingly close to him for a while as she roamed around the room touching the marble and terracotta figures with light fingertips, and remembering. The bust of the village child he had been working on when he died was still wrapped in its protective cloths, but they had dried out now, she noticed, and it was a sharp reminder that the figure was never going to be finished. Such a sharp reminder that for a moment she felt the pain of his loss all over again, and bit hard on her bottom lip.

The painting of her mother still hung on the wall, barely discernible in the shadowy moonlight, but what features she could not actually see, she could fill in from memory. The almost sly look in the eyes and the mouth with its sensual half-smile, as if she shared a secret with the artist who had been her husband and Bethany's father. The mysterious Apollo who had drifted briefly back into her life and out again, without even identifying himself.

She recalled the man himself and the marble reproduction of those stunningly handsome features as one impression; then wondered why Papa had never immortalised Megan in marble as Megan had done her handsome first husband. Or perhaps that had been his reason for not doing so. She thought of Papa's hurt when Megan returned to her Apollo and how he had wept, and she was so deeply engrossed in the secret and selfish behaviour of her natural parents that she heard nothing until a voice spoke her name softly in the shadowy moonlight.

'Bethany?'

Swinging round quickly, she stared with her mouth open and breathed as in panic, for the voice was deep and soft and brought a curious sense of anticipation that she did not begin to understand. She looked and felt very small standing there in her plain cotton nightgown with her feet bare and her tawny hair tossed and rumpled from trying to get to sleep.

Nikolas stood just behind her, his lean length wrapped in a cotton robe that stopped short just below his knees and showed long brown legs and bare feet. His hair too was rumpled and it gave him a much less severe look than usual that was comforting in the present circumstances. She looked at him warily for the first few moments while she tried to still the almost choking urgency of her heartbeat.

'I couldn't sleep,' she explained, in a small voice that was little more than a whisper but seemed somehow to find an echo in the shadowy corners of the room.

'You've had rather a shattering day,' Nikolas reminded her, and the unmistakable sympathy in his voice reminded her of how he had brought her most of the way home held close in the curve of his arm. 'You must try not to brood on things you can't change, Bethany. It's over and done with and I don't imagine Apollo is ever going to appear again to trouble you.'

How could she tell him that in one small corner of her heart she wished he would? Instead she nodded jerkily, her tawny head bowed as she studied her bare toes peeping out from below the hem of her nightgown. 'I don't suppose he will,' she agreed, then looked up at him and smiled ruefully. 'Couldn't you sleep either, Niko?' The familiar use of his name seemed more and more natural to her lately, and she liked its suggestion of intimacy.

'I heard something.'

She could just make out the gleaming darkness of his eyes and for some reason was reminded of the night he had brought her home from her moonlight swim. It seemed scarcely credible that it was such a short time ago and she wondered if he remembered it as vividly as she did. A gleam of white teeth confirmed the fact that he was smiling, and she remembered hazily that his room was almost immediately above the studio.

'I'm sorry,' she murmured. 'I tried not to wake anyone.'

'You didn't wake me, I was already awake or I probably wouldn't even have heard you.' He took a step nearer and stood looking down at her face for a moment; creamy pale in the moonlight and with the grey eyes shadowed by their heavy lashes to a darkness almost as deep as his own. 'I suspected it might be——' He seemed to have second thoughts about what he had started to say, and shook his head slowly. 'You might have been a thief who'd broken in.'

'We don't have that kind of trouble here,' she told him, wishing that she did not tremble so much or that she did not have such an aching desire to be held in his arms and comforted. There was no possible reason why she should need that kind of comforting, but still the feeling persisted and she shook her head, impatient with herself. 'Where would a thief run to in Apolidus?'

she asked with a shivery little laugh. 'Everyone here is known to everyone else, except when someone occasionally comes from outside, like Theo.' She broke off there because it suddenly occurred to her what he was going to say when he told her he suspected it might be—and stopped himself there. 'You thought Theo might be here, didn't you, Nikolas?'

The words came almost of their own volition and she bit hard on her lower lip while she waited for him to answer her. It was instinctive when she closed her eyes briefly and he reached out and took her chin in his hand, holding her so that a shaft of moonlight from the window fell directly across her face. His fingers were hard and strong, but their hold was more suggestive of a caress than of force as they curved into her jaw.

'I wouldn't have been surprised to find him here,' he agreed, and Bethany took heed of the edge on his voice even though it was barely above a whisper. 'I'm only thankful that I didn't find you together—does that answer your question?'

Her heart was thudding heavily, and she was alarmed to realise how easy it would be to become angry with him, when only seconds ago she had been longing to be in his arms. 'In fact what you mean is that you believe I might be here to see him!' There was something infinitely disturbing about standing there in the moonlit studio with him, just as there had been about that first time on the moonlit hillside, and she found herself speculating on the possibility of being kissed again as she had been that night. 'Oh, Niko,' she whispered, 'why should you think that? Don't you trust me?'

She half expected him to become angry, but instead he lifted a strand of her hair and let it run through his fingers like silken threads on to her bare shoulders, and she shivered slightly. 'It's Theo I didn't trust,' he confessed with obvious unwillingness. 'I know his dislike of losing when he's set his heart on getting something he particularly wants.'

'But he wouldn't come here.'

Bethany wasn't sure whether she believed that or not, but obviously Nikolas had no doubt at all, and he was nodding his head. 'Oh, but he would, child—for you.'

It was curious, the feeling she had as she stood there listening to him declare his brother quite capable of sneaking out of his room at the *taverna* to come and see her. Not simply to see her, Bethany knew, she was not so naïve, and she remembered Theo's jibe about Nikolas protecting his ewe lamb from the wolves, and Nikolas's ready admission of it. Theo would find such protectiveness an irresistible challenge.

She never quite knew why she glanced beyond him to the wide, uncurtained window when she did. But she caught sight of a mere glimpse of movement in the garden beyond, and for a second or two she stared at the gleaming darkness of the glass as if she was mesmerised. There was a wild thud of panic in her heartbeat suddenly, and she realised that Nikolas had turned and was following the direction of her gaze.

'What is it?' he asked, and his hand on her shoulder was warm and reassuring. 'Bethany?'

'Nothing—nothing really.' She sounded breathless and she knew it, for a persistent niggle of suspicion had her on edge. 'I saw one of the bushes move, that's all. The wind's getting up, I think; probably the *meltémi*, and we'll have a storm.'

Her heart was hammering and she did not know what to say or how to react. It had to be Theo she had glimpsed through the window, and it was unlikely he had seen them in the room, therefore he would probably come closer and try to get in. Nikolas had said he would not let anything stand in his way if he had made up his mind, and somehow she had to turn him away.

If Nikolas knew he was there he would either revert to his former suspicion, that she had come down to let Theo in, or there would be a terrible quarrel between them, which was equally undesirable. Into a torment of indecision Nikolas's voice intruded, soft and deep and infinitely affecting.

'You should be in bed and asleep,' he told her, and again his long fingers rippled through her hair.

But sleep had never been further from her mind, and Bethany still sought desperately for a solution. 'It's so oppressive,' she said in a small, husky voice, 'I'm sure it's going to storm, Niko. I'd—I'd love to go outside for a few minutes.' She felt alarmingly breathless as she took the path of deception and prayed she did not become trapped in her own deceit.

'In your nightgown?' Nikolas asked, and sounded faintly amused rather than shocked, so that she coloured furiously and thanked heaven for the semi-darkness of the studio so that he could not see her too clearly. 'And with nothing on your feet?'

'Just outside,' she coaxed, stunned by her own deviousness and a little ashamed of it too. 'Or maybe if I could just open a window and sit on the sill for a couple of minutes.'

'You're a strange child!' His tone was indulgent, and she smiled up at him when he leaned past her to open the window wide. Perching himself on the window ledge beside her, he looked up at the moon with a faintly quizzical eye. 'Moon madness,' he teased softly, and a low ripple of laugher sent tiny thrills all along her spine. 'Just a few minutes, and then we will both go back to bed and try to sleep.'

'Just a few minutes,' Bethany agreed.

There was a curious sense of peace and contentment sitting there with him in the moonlight, so that she almost forgot for a moment or two the reason for her insistence. If Theo did not see them now in the full light of the moon and leave before he was seen, he would be very stupid, and she did not believe that of him. Her nightgown was white and showed up as clearly as Nikolas's light robe did, so that Theo could not fail to know that she was not there alone.

Briefly she thought she caught sight of another glimpse of movement off to their left, but she tried not to show anything in her manner, and fortunately it was out of Nikolas's line of vision as he sat sideways on the windowsill. A momentary flutter of movement among the shrubs and it was gone. The message, she thought, had been seen and understood and she heaved an inward sigh of relief. She also felt curiously certain suddenly that she was never going to marry Theo; although she did not stop to ask herself at the moment why she had come to a decision so abruptly. Something about this particular situation must have decided her.

She caught her breath audibly when a few moments later a hand was placed on her arm and strong fingers pressed into her flesh. 'You're getting chilled,' Nikolas said in a tone she knew well. 'It's time you went back to bed.' He closed the window carefully and quietly, then turned to face her for a moment. 'I can't think why I indulged such a crazy, childish notion,' he told her, and sounded almost as if he mused his private thoughts aloud. 'You'll go back to your room, young lady, and into bed and stay there until morning—the idea!'

Bethany's small trill of laughter was irresistible, for she had not for a moment believed he would indulge her so far or so readily, and the satisfaction it gave her far outweighed the importance of sending Theo scuttling back to the *taverna*. Stretching her arms above her head, she yawned sleepily. 'I think I might sleep now,' she said.

There was no window on the staircase and he took her arm as they went up the stairs, holding her to the comforting warmth of him in the almost total darkness. They were at the top of the stairs, on the narrow landing, when she recalled her firm decision about Theo, and she looked up at Nikolas from the corner of her eye, moving closer so that she need not raise her voice above a whisper.

'Nikolas, you won't insist on me marrying Theo, will you? You did promise that I needn't marry anyone I didn't love.'

His brief silence puzzled her rather, so that for a moment she wondered if he was displeased at her decision. Then once more his fingers pressed hard into her soft flesh and his breath was warm against her neck when he bent to whisper his reply close to her ear. 'Don't you want to marry Theo?' he asked, and she shook her head as well as she could for his proximity.

'No!' she replied with certainty, and again the hand on her arm squeezed hard.

'Then you shan't, little one,' he assured her in a whisper that nevertheless carried the assurance of authority.

They came to a halt outside her bedroom door and she instinctively turned towards him, her mouth already soft and yielding, anticipating the kiss she had been thinking about ever since he came into the studio. There was a shivering excitement in the body that seemed to exude its own heat in the narrow passageway and made her tremble, but he did not take her in his arms.

'Goodnight, Bethany; make sure you go to bed and go to sleep!'

'Goodnight!'

It was hard to accept that he meant simply to send her to bed like a naughty little girl, and she looked up at him, trying to determine the expression he wore, but could define only the deep darkness of his eyes. A small window let in a little of the moonlight and in the shadowy haze he looked incredibly tall and vaguely Oriental, that hint of his mother's Turkish blood in the cast of his features and slightly almond eyes. He could have turned and gone, but he hesitated, and a thrill of excitement scuttled along her back like a ripple of cool silk because of it.

She laughed softly and a little wildly, thinking again of Theo sneaking back to the *taverna*, and her heart was beating so hard she felt alarmingly breathless. 'Why do I feel so wicked?' she whispered, and saw the white gleam of Nikolas's smile for a moment.

'Why indeed?' he asked with a hint of irony.

He bent his head to kiss her lightly beside her mouth, and Bethany was never quite sure why it went further than that. It could surely not have been because she lifted her arms and put them around his neck that he pulled her to him suddenly and sought her mouth with a passionate eagerness she could not have resisted even had she been of a mind to.

He had never kissed her mouth before other than in anger, and the sensation was startlingly different. The hard passionate mouth sought hungrily for her response, and buried itself deep in hers, while his arms pressed her with urgent desire to a masculinity only thinly disguised by the light robe he wore. It was as if she had been cut off from all contact with reality, and she felt the urgent response of her own body as something she had no control over. Her feet seemed not to touch the ground, but it was only when her toes gently touched down on the rough matting again that she realised he had literally swept her off her feet.

Looking up, she regretted not being able to see his face more clearly, but his big hands slid slowly from her body in a long sweeping caress, then were cupped either side of her face, the thumbs pressing lightly on her lips. He bent closer so that he need not raise his voice and the soft skin of her neck fluttered with each word.

'Go back to bed, Bethany, please!'

Tipping back her head, she looked up into his face and noted the gleaming darkness of his eyes. Then a sudden wild and inexplicable feeling flooded through her whole body, bringing sensations she found hard to control; exciting but alarming sensations that urged her towards something she did not yet want to recognise, and she stepped away from him, turning quickly to open her bedroom door.

'Goodnight!' The words tumbled from her lips and she stepped quickly through and closed the door.

# CHAPTER EIGHT

IT had been almost daylight before Bethany went to sleep, for the excitement of those few moments with Nikolas had kept her awake, wide-eyed and glowing, until sheer tiredness closed her eyes. But the feeling was still with her when she woke, a feeling so lighthearted and filled with anticipation that she hummed a tune to herself as she went downstairs to help with breakfast.

Apart from the fact that Nikolas had kissed her goodnight, she kept telling herself that nothing had really happened to make her feel as she did, and yet nothing, it seemed, could touch her with discontent this morning. By now Nikolas must have realised that his confidence regarding Papa's choice of a husband for her had been passed on, and he must be aware of who her informant was too, but such was her mood that Bethany could not believe he would blame his aunt for telling her. He knew how she felt about Theo too, and surely no man who had kissed a woman as Nikolas had kissed her last night could later turn around and insist that she marry someone else, particularly his own brother.

It occurred to her vaguely that Alexia was perhaps a little less communicative than usual, but it probably meant simply that Alexia had also had a restless night and was feeling a little under par. Together they prepared breakfast and, wrapped as she was in her own sunny mood, Bethany did not mind at all being left with her own thoughts.

It was more or less routine by now that Nikolas had his breakfast alone in the first place, because he was always first at table, then Alexia and Bethany joined him shortly afterwards and they finished the meal together. Takis invariably appeared late and gobbled down his meal at the very last minute, when it was almost time to leave for school.

Today as Bethany carried the tray across the terrace to where Nikolas sat at the table under the plane tree, she found herself taking explicit note of every detail. The way he leaned one elbow on the table with his chin resting on the hand as he read through the papers that always arrived on the morning ferry for him, and the way a deep cream shirt pulled taut across broad shoulders showing the shadow of a lean brown back through its texture. The way his hair grew in a slight curl above his ears, sable dark but flecked with a suggestion of silver if you caught it in a certain light; a gentle reminder of his thirty-odd years.

There was an arrogance about him that she had hated in those first turbulent days when he had represented an intrusion into her comfortable little haven; now it seemed sometimes as if he had always been there. He seemed to fit in, unlike Theo whose lusty and mischievous temperament seemed completely alien to the quiet peace of Apolidus.

Bringing Theo to mind had an immediate and slightly cooling effect on her glowing good humour, for Theo, she remembered, could do a great deal to spoil things for her if he was of a mind to. He must have known, or at least guessed, the reason for that charade in the studio window last night, and she could only pray that he was discreet enough to say nothing.

Nikolas must have heard her coming, for he turned when she was less than half way across the stone-paved terrace, and came to relieve her of the tray, as he most often did. Taking stock of her flushed cheeks and bright shining eyes, he smiled, faintly quizzical, as he set the tray down on the table.

'Did you get some sleep after all?' he asked.

Having put down the tray, he left pouring out the coffee to her, sitting down again and watching her, still with that slightly sardonic smile, one elbow resting on the table and tapping a light tattoo on its surface. It crossed Bethany's mind to tell him how long she had lain awake, unable to sleep for the excitement he had aroused in her, but instead she simply nodded and smiled.

'Yes, thank you, Nikolas, did you?' He nodded as she handed him his coffee, and she went on, 'I just needed some fresh air, that was all.'

'Don't you have a window in your bedroom?' he asked, amusement lurking deep in his eyes. 'Or are you in the habit of prowling around down there in the early hours of the morning?'

'You'd have discovered it if I was, long before now!' Bethany retorted, but without malice.

She felt oddly nervous and there was a tingling sensation at her nerve-ends that made her want to shiver. She wished she had not deceived him last night about seeing someone outside in the garden. Almost certainly it had been Theo, especially since Nikolas himself had been half expecting to find him there when he came downstairs, and she was too unsure of his brother's reaction.

'Sit down,' Nikolas urged, more serious suddenly. 'There's something I have to say to you before Aunt Alexia joins us.' Bethany's heart lurched sickeningly, but she told herself that Theo could not possibly have seen him yet, and if he had and Nikolas was still in a good humour, then she had nothing to worry about. He looked at the tray, set only for one. 'Didn't you bring yourself a cup?'

'Well, no, I was going to have mine later, but——' She was already half turned to go and fetch herself a cup when he stopped her.

'No, it will take too much time, and I want to say what I have to say before we're interrupted.' Trembling slightly, Bethany sat and watched him while he spread a roll with butter and honey, then handed it to her with a glimmer of a smile. 'That will sustain you for the moment, you can have some coffee later.'

Bethany nibbled the roll absently but did not take her eyes off his face, shadowed and, it seemed, oddly secretive. 'Niko, what's wrong?'

There was something, she told herself, or why else

would he want to say something to her before Alexia came out to join them as she always did? Yet again she rued her inability to sit at the same table with him and think rationally. It was hard to concentrate on what he was going to say when she was so fascinated by the firm sureness of his hands, reminding her of how tenderly they had held her last night.

'Last night,' Nikolas began, and brought her swiftly back to earth because from the way he hesitated it seemed he might be unsure of what he wanted to say, and that wasn't like Nikolas at all. His uncertainty was shortlived, however, and he pressed on as if impatient with his own reticence. 'Aunt Alexia heard you go downstairs last night, Bethany, and she heard me go down shortly afterwards.' Bethany waited. 'She also heard us come back up together,' Nikolas went on, 'and she saw me kiss you.'

Bethany's heart was rapping urgently because there was something in his voice that set every nerve in her body tingling, and she kept the thick tawny lashes lowered over her eyes. Vaguely she recalled Alexia's quietness earlier on, and realised how shocked the old lady must have been to see Nikolas, to whom she attributed all the traditional virtues, kissing the girl he had hinted himself was intended for his brother's bride. But she was much more concerned to know what Nikolas might have told her by way of an explanation, and prayed desperately that he wasn't going to pass the incident off as merely a lighthearted caress that meant nothing at all. She didn't think she could bear that.

Nikolas was looking at her steadily and there was something in his eyes that brought all those wild and almost frightening emotions flooding back, just like last night outside her bedroom door. It enveloped her in an indescribable need for him, a physical need that was alarming in its fierceness and made her feel far too emotional to think clearly.

'Bethany, I had to tell her——'

'Good morning!'

Bethany gasped aloud when Theo's brightly loud

voice cut across what Nikolas had been trying to say,
and Bethany did not remember ever resenting anyone
as much as she did Theo at that moment. He sat down
beside her and gave her a wide and faintly malicious
smile, although she could not for the moment account
for the malice. Then she remembered, and glanced
swiftly at Nikolas.

'Good morning, Theo.' Nikolas spread another roll,
quite unperturbed it seemed, until Bethany noticed
how hard he gripped the knife handle. 'Was your room
comfortable?'

Theo filched a morsel of roll and honey from
Bethany's plate and popped it into his mouth before he
answered, and there was a bright gleam in his eyes that
she found infinitely disturbing. 'Well enough,' he said,
and caught Nikolas's eye, narrowing his own. 'Was
yours?'

Briefly Nikolas glanced at Bethany then back again
to his brother, while Bethany prayed as she never had
in her life before. But he said nothing and after a
second or two Theo shrugged with what was obviously
assumed carelessness. Even in a situation like this, when
he could so easily have had the upper hand, it seemed
he was prepared to back down, though Bethany was
still on tenterhooks.

'Have I your permission to take our cousin swimming this morning?' Theo asked, and there was a definite edge of challenge on the question that made
Bethany glance at him sharply. 'You like swimming,
don't you, cousin?'

She couldn't deny it, but quite unconsciously she
had glanced at Nikolas before she nodded agreement,
and her answer was clearly not as eager as Theo expected. 'I—I suppose I could go,' she said, 'but later,
Theo, when all the chores are done and I have some
time to spare.'

'You may be taking a holiday,' Nikolas told him in a
deep and much too quiet voice, 'but no one else is,
Theo. Bethany has work to do, she hasn't the time to
keep you amused all day long.'

'Oh, Nikolas!' Her reproach was soft-voiced, but a stirring of the old resentment showed for a moment in her eyes. 'It wouldn't matter for a little while, surely, when I've finished what I have to do in the house, and I do like swimming. Please—be reasonable!'

He disliked her pleading with him, she could see it in the way he looked at her, and she could not understand his being so conventional about her going with Theo for a little while when there would be no one about to condemn their being unaccompanied. His response showed her in what direction his mind was working and stunned her with its unexpectedness.

'Were you thinking of taking a swimsuit with you?' Nikolas asked in a voice that was scarcely above a whisper, and Bethany felt the colour flooding into her face.

Theo must have caught the words, however softly spoken, and they obviously intrigued him although he said nothing for the moment. Bethany, however, was shaking with some emotion she could not recognise and trying to understand why he should raise such a matter at this particular moment.

'You——' She licked her dry lips, finding the words hard to come by. 'You dare to suggest that I'd——'

'I dare?' Nikolas echoed, and she shivered at the narrowed darkness of his eyes fixed on her so steadily. For in them she seemed to see her own nakedly pale form emerging from the moonlit sea to find him standing there on the beach, waiting for her. 'I'm your guardian, but it seems I need to remind you of it, yet again!'

'Niko!'

She could have cried, only she wouldn't let him see how much he could affect her. She had no idea what he had been going to say when Theo interrupted him earlier, but quite obviously he disliked not only his brother's inopportune arrival, but also her readiness to go swimming with him. Strangely though, his reaction did not anger her, only gave her a curious kind of thrill that mingled confusingly with the hurt she felt.

'You must know I wouldn't,' she whispered, and

gazed at him in disbelief when he evaded her eyes suddenly. It was strange how she got the impression that for the first time since she had known him, she had the upper hand, though she had no idea how it had come about. 'Niko?'

'Holy Mother!' Again Theo's impatient voice cut into a curiously intimate moment, proclaiming his annoyance at not getting his own way without opposition. 'Don't you take your eyes off her, even to sleep?' he demanded. 'Do you stand guard in the small hours too, ready to repel all comers?' He got to his feet, seemingly unaware of the almost tangible air of tension between them and concerned only with his own ineffable frustration. 'A man could die of boredom on your precious little island, cousin!' he informed Bethany. 'And it wouldn't take twenty-four hours!'

Neither Nikolas nor Bethany said anything, and after a moment Theo gave an impatient snort of disgust and turned away, marching off across the terrace the way he had come, his tall figure tense with anger and frustration. The moment he was out of sight, Nikolas got up, and as he stood for a moment with both hands clasped behind him and his back to her, Bethany felt the urgent, anxious beat of her heart drowning out every other sound. Maybe Theo had not intended to make mischief, but there was only one way that Nikolas could interpret his words, and Bethany waited for the storm to break.

'He was here and you knew it!'

He spoke without turning round, and Bethany pressed her hands together anxiously. It wasn't easy to explain why she had deceived him last night, and the sight of that broad back turned on her did not help at all. She felt too vulnerable and much too insignificant sitting down, and got to her feet.

'You *did* know, didn't you?'

He swung around so swiftly that she took an involuntary step backwards. It wasn't so much a question as a statement of fact, as if he had no doubt at all he was right, and Bethany wondered what on earth she could say that would not make matters worse. After the trouble she had gone to to prevent him finding out about Theo, it was ironic that she should be left to face the music alone.

'I—I don't know how to explain,' she confessed in a small and very unsteady voice.

'But you knew he was there last night—outside somewhere?'

'I knew—I thought someone was out there.' She ventured a compromise, but it failed as she had known it would.

'Damn it, Bethany, you *knew* it had to be Theo!' His mouth had contracted into a firm hard line, while Bethany's in contrast looked soft and very vulnerable. 'And you contrived that little pantomime at the window to let him know I was with you and that the coast wasn't clear!'

'*No!*'

The harsh bark of laughter he gave sent shivers fluttering along her spine so that she crossed her arms over her breast and shook her head slowly. 'And I was readily persuaded, wasn't I, Bethany? So ready to indulge your whim and sit there in the window with you!'

It was hard to believe, judging on his voice alone, that there was hurt as well as anger in his eyes, and Bethany felt a lump in her throat that refused to be swallowed. If it took all the persuasion she was capable of, she had to convince him that she hadn't known Theo was coming.

'I caught sight of something—someone outside,' she told him huskily. 'I couldn't be sure it was Theo.' Once more he laughed in that hard, humourless way that made her wince as from a blow. 'I wasn't there to *meet* him, Nikolas, you must believe me!'

'Did I spoil your plans completely?' He ignored her denials and seemed to get some kind of relief out of berating her so ruthlessly. 'Or did he come back later, after I'd left you?'

As if she had even given Theo a thought, with her

mouth still tingling from Nikolas's kiss, and feeling as she never had before, with that curious and frightening sensation surging through her body like a fire that threatened to consume her. She hadn't given anyone a thought except Nikolas, and she had relived those few passionate moments in his arms over and over until she fell asleep.

'You know he didn't come back, Niko,' she whispered, and there was nothing she could do now about the tears that streamed down her face. 'And if he had you know I wouldn't have seen him. You know I *couldn't*!'

She tried with every fibre of her being to remind him of that kiss, but perhaps he was too accustomed to such moments to treasure it as she had since last night. She was more hurt than angry, even now, and she could think only of how thrillingly passionate that angry mouth had been when he kissed her, and how willingly she had responded to it.

'But I don't expect you to admit that you could be wrong,' she went on when he stood silently with one hand rubbing at the back of his head and the other spanned over his right hip. 'Nor do I expect you to apologise for misjudging me, Nikolas. You always have right on your side as you've often reminded me; not only right but might too, it seems! I——'

The need to hurt back had driven her thus far, but she couldn't go on and she swallowed hard, incapable of saying another word. Then she turned swiftly and ran back to the house, almost colliding with Takis on his way to eat breakfast.

He looked at her in some surprise when she did not even answer his greeting, but went straight on upstairs, and as she flopped down on to her bed she hated Theo with a virulence she had never thought herself capable of. She certainly would not marry him, no matter what anyone said to try and persuade her. How could she when it was Nikolas who could lift her to the heights or dash her to the ground merely with a few words?

It was only when Theo announced his intention of leaving and going back home to Rhodes that Bethany felt a vague prickle of conscience because she had not made him more welcome. Alexia clearly did not know what to believe, but she had a soft spot for Theo and she would have liked him to stay longer, so would Takis.

'I'm a fish out of water, dear aunt,' Theo told her with his blandest smile. 'This quiet little island isn't my scene at all, though I'm sure it's a perfect paradise for those who like that sort of thing.'

'I wouldn't change it for all the islands in the Aegean,' Bethany told him, staunchly partisan as always, and Theo smiled, letting a strand of her hair slip through his fingers.

'I know you say so now, cousin,' he said, and his eyes had a curiously speculative look as he watched her. 'But suppose some day you have to choose?' She frowned at him. 'Between your island and a man you love,' Theo suggested. 'Who'd win *that* contest, I wonder, Beth, eh?'

'Apolidus without doubt,' Bethany assured him. 'I couldn't even begin to love a man who didn't like Apolidus.'

'Like, cousin,' Theo pointed out very seriously, 'is much different from being prepared to give up everything we've come to think of as civilised and stay here forever. Don't you realise that?'

In some curious way he seemed very like Nikolas at that moment, and Bethany felt an affection for him that she had never even come close to before. 'I still think that if he loved me enough he'd stay,' she told him, and it was strange how certain she was that they were both talking about Nikolas. Not only strange but disconcerting.

'And you, sweet cousin?' Theo asked softly, rippling her tawny hair through his fingers still. 'Would you give up your island—if you loved him enough?'

Her heart thudded hard and Bethany knew the colour was in her cheeks, but she determinedly put the

idea of their hypothetical lover out of her mind. Aware
that Alexia too was watching her, and thanking heaven
that Nikolas wasn't there to hear them, she shook her
head. 'I couldn't,' she said. 'I couldn't give up Apolidus
for anyone, it's—it's my haven, Theo; my—my security.'

It seemed odd to be talking to Theo like that, and
she jumped up after a brief glance at the mantel clock.
Alexia glanced at it too and looked unhappy, taking
Theo's hands as he prepared to go. 'It would have
been good for you to stay longer, Theo,' she told him.
'Come again, eh?'

Theo wrapped his strong young arms around her
shoulders and hugged her close, pressing his smooth
cheek to hers. 'Better you come to us, dearest aunt,' he
told her, and kissed her affectionately, beaming her his
most persuasive smile. '*Au revoir*, dear aunt, come to
us soon!'

To compensate in some way for her lack of welcome
Bethany walked with Theo down to the ferry a few
minutes later, and did not bother to ask whether
Nikolas approved or not. He had said nothing when
she announced her intention, but bade his brother an
affectionate goodbye, neither of them showing a trace
of animosity, and their near-quarrel of that morning
apparently forgotten. It was typical of Greek temperament, Bethany thought with a rare essay into her native
character, that such fierce anger could so soon be forgotten.

Theo was quiet as he walked beside her carrying his
light overnight bag, and she could not help but admit
that she liked him better when he was being less arrogantly demanding. They said little until they were
half-way along the path leading to the harbour, then
Theo turned his head suddenly and caught her eye.

He winked solemnly and she had to hastily control
an urge to laugh aloud, a control that slipped completely when he pulled a face at her. Reaching for her
hand, he squeezed her fingers so hard that she gasped,
then raised them to his lips and kissed each one lightly

while they walked down the stony path together.

'Forgive me?' he asked, and Bethany had no need to ask that he referred to his betrayal of their secret that morning. He must have realised how angry Nikolas would be, whether or not he had said anything to him about it afterwards. 'I wouldn't have said anything to make trouble between you and Niko if I'd known, you must know that.' He kissed her fingers lightly once more before letting them go. 'But I didn't know, though I suppose I should have.'

'What didn't you know?' Bethany asked, but in asking the question it seemed she provided the answer, and she was shaking her head to deny the need for confirmation even before he began.

'That it's Niko you—care about,' said Theo, and smiled faintly when colour flooded into her cheeks. 'I'm sorry, Beth; forget I said that, hmm?'

Bethany said nothing for the moment, but a gamut of emotions whirled and tangled through her brain until she found it hard to think clearly about anything at all. She had to skip to keep pace with Theo, and the wind tugged at her tawny hair, blowing it out behind her and keeping the warm bright colour alive in her cheeks. There was enough similarity in Theo to bring something of the same reaction from her, although nothing like the depth of emotion that Nikolas aroused.

She noticed how tall and straight he was, and how his head was carried with a natural arrogance. A profile, more handsome than Nikolas, but with the same suggestion of a figure cast in bronze, strong and very masculine, displayed against a background of sea and hot blue sky.

'Will we see you again, Theo?'

He turned his head and the wind lifted thick black hair, tossing it back from a broad brow, and again he pulled a face. 'I'm not very taken with your island, cousin, so I doubt whether I'll ever come back to it.'

'Oh, but you haven't given it a chance!' Bethany protested. 'It's beautiful. Theo, the most beautiful in the Aegean, or anywhere, and I shall never leave it!'

His hand squeezed hard, and he was very sober suddenly, his eyes heavy-lidded as he regarded her steadily. 'Oh, Beth,' he said softly, 'I think you will.'

'Never!'

She was so sure, and yet when she remembered their conversation earlier she wondered if he knew something she did not. Nikolas had said during their first visit to Rhodes, that he would be going back there and taking them all with him. Takis would certainly go, to his new school, and Aunt Alexia she knew would readily go back to her own home; Nikolas's feelings could never be in dispute and it would be him, she realised, whom she would have to persuade if she was ever allowed to stay in Apolidus.

For the moment she thrust the problem from her mind and concentrated on more immediate matters, finding them much less disturbing. Below against the harbour wall, a small shabby caique bounced on the turning tide, having disgorged the cargo from the squat belly of its hold, and the urgency now was for it to be off again. The captain and his crew, fortified with a friendly glass of *raki* in the *taverna*, were waiting.

It was doubtful if there had been any passengers, for there seldom were passengers to Apolidus, only occasionally someone coming to visit relatives, as Theo had. Walking along the cobbled quay, Theo let go her hand again, as if he guessed that news of Pavlos Meandis's daughter walking hand in hand with the *xenos* would cheerfully be handed round the *taverna* that evening with the *raki*. Neither of them doubted that Theo's identity was known to every man, woman and child on the island, no matter how short his stay had been, and such intimacy would be grounds for speculation.

'I wonder if there's any post,' said Bethany. 'Nikolas has most of it, of course, but occasionally Aunt Alex has a letter from her sister or a friend.'

'Don't you ever get any?' Theo asked, and she shook her head.

'Who'd write to me?' she asked, seeing nothing extra-ordinary in the situation, and Theo shook his head slowly, as if he found it hard to believe.

'How do you survive such complete isolation?' he asked, and when she smiled. 'Even your ferry is ancient and almost falling to pieces.'

'Oh, nonsense!' Bethany denied, laughing at what she considered an exaggeration. 'You'd better not let Captain Spiros hear you say that, either!'

She laughed gleefully at the very idea of little in-offensive Captain Spiros challenging someone like Theo on any matter at all, and Theo moved a little closer, taking hold of her fingers again, though very discreetly. 'You look beautiful when you laugh,' he told her, and his dark eyes moved in rapt and frank admiration over her slightly flushed face. 'What a glorious bride you'll make, little cousin.'

As Bethany turned her head to look at him, her heart was clamouring so hard it almost deafened her, and she stared at Theo with a glimmer of wariness in her eyes. 'A—a bride?'

Theo's dark brows winged upward, as if her question surprised him. 'But of course; you don't plan to remain single all your life, do you?' His glowing eyes once more traversed her features in a way that made her colour rise. 'You don't imagine any red-blooded man will allow such a thing to happen, do you? Least of all Niko!'

'But——' Bethany swallowed hard, because it was suddenly very hard to think clearly. 'Nikolas promised that he wouldn't insist on me marrying someone I didn't love,' she reminded him.

'And nor will he, sweet cousin,' Theo assured her with a smile.

'And I've told him that I won't—I don't want to—I mean—I can't marry you, Theo.' She felt horribly anxious suddenly and her tongue flicked nervously across dry lips as she watched his darkly handsome features for some sign of what he was getting at.

But he merely looked at her from the corner of his

eyes and half smiled. 'I never imagined you would, Beth,' he told her.

Quite confused, she frowned at him uncertainly. 'You didn't?'

'You don't love *me*, do you?' he asked, but it was clearly not a serious question, and she shook her head automatically. Then he smiled and there was a warmth in his eyes that reminded her of Nikolas in his gentler moments. 'And fortunately, I don't love you, my sweet little cousin, so I'm not likely to raise any objections. There was never any question of you marrying *me*.'

'But——' She shook her head in confusion. 'Aunt Alex said——'

Theo merely smiled, as if he knew a great deal more about the subject they were discussing than she did herself, but there was no time for her to say anything more, for a small wizened man in a peak cap was hurrying along the quay towards them and holding an envelope in one hand which he waved like a flag as he came.

'*Thespinís!* Thespinís Meandis! A letter for you from Athens! See the postmark!'

He was blowing hard and his brown wrinkled face was shiny with perspiration, and as he came to a halt in front of her, Bethany looked at him in disbelief. The man's broken teeth beamed in a satisfied smile, for who better than he to know that the daughter of Pavlos Meandis had never before received any mail? Placing the precious missive in her hands, along with one for Nikolas, he beamed at her.

'There, *thespinís*! And one also for Kírios Meandis.'

Bethany could scarcely believe it until she saw her own name scrawled in large bold script on a plain white envelope, and Theo was watching her with a faintly quizzical smile. 'Who'd write to you?' he reminded her, and Bethany shrugged, still hardly convinced. 'Who do you know in Athens, Bethany?'

It occurred to her vaguely that he sounded rather like Nikolas when he used that interrogative tone, and she shook her head. 'No one; I mean—I can't think of anyone.'

But while she stood there holding the thin white envelope in her hands she began to get the strangest feeling about it. Impulsively and with Theo watching her, she slipped a finger along under the flap of the envelope and opened it, taking out a single sheet of paper. It was folded in half and written in the same big, bold script that appeared on the envelope—and it was in English.

Her eyes went at once to the signature at the foot of the page and she saw through suddenly hazy eyes the name written there, and smiled. Refolding it carefully, she placed it back in the envelope with hands that were not quite steady, aware that Theo was still waiting, and expecting, to be enlightened.

'Well?' he prompted, and Bethany looked up at him and smiled, rather absently, although she did not realise it.

Once more it was Captain Spiros who forestalled an explanation, for he was already back on board and waited only for his single passenger to join them before he gave the order to sail. Theo was unaccustomed to having to consider other people's timetables, and as he seemed not to have noticed that he was holding up the ferry's departure, Bethany touched a hand to his elbow to remind him, when the boat's klaxon blew.

'You must hurry, Theo, you're holding up the ferry.'

Theo glanced over his shoulder impatiently, but he had little option but to move along with her towards the little caique's heaving gangway, though he stood at the foot of it instead of going aboard, still more interested in who her letter was from than in any urgency of the ferry's captain.

'You must go, Theo, really!' Bethany tiptoed impulsively and kissed his cheek. So much for discretion, but she was not in a mood to consider gossip at the moment, nor to notice the eye-rolling among the men in the boats anchored nearby. 'Have a good journey, Theo! Be happy!'

'Bethany——'

'*Kirie, kirie*, hurry if you please! We leave at once!'

Caught between two stools, Theo turned back and

forth between them, then eventually saw no alternative and shrugged resignedly before he turned to take the swaying gangplank in long awkward strides. He was barely on board before it was pulled in after him, but he stood in the opening it had left, looking at Bethany on shore. Surrounded by slapping lines on deck and the noisy chug of the caique's engine as it came reluctantly to life with a choking stench of diesel fumes, Theo frowned.

He stepped back hastily when one of the crew swung the hinged rail into place over the gap, then called something to Bethany above the clamour of the engine and the authoritative bellow of the captain in the door of his wheelhouse. 'Who is it, Bethany?'

It was impossible not to smile at his insistence, and there was really no need for secrecy, so she sent the answer after him as she waved her hand. The words were half lost in the noise and the brisk wind that slapped into his face the moment the caique began to move.

'My father!' Bethany called to him. 'It's from my father!'

# CHAPTER NINE

'*Bethany, I may call you that because it was I who chose your name, the name you have kept even though you took your stepfather's surname.*'

Bethany read the words for the hundredth time, sitting curled up on the small bed that had been hers for as long as she could remember. The big bold writing was in some ways oddly similar to Papa's, and that struck her as odd when she had always thought of the two men as so dissimilar.

'*I should have at least had the courage to tell you who I was when I spoke with you that evening, and to ask for your forgiveness,*' the letter went on, '*but courage was never my strong point, and you so clearly despised the man you knew only by reputation. Who could blame you? Your stepfather was obviously so much more worthy of your love, but I would ask you now to forgive me, Bethany, and perhaps sometimes try to think a little more kindly than you have to date, of the man who fathered you. No doubt Pavlos Meandis was more worthy of your love, but having seen you I realise what might have been. May the gods protect you, daughter. Apollo (Michael Apollo Scott).*'

Bethany knew the words almost by heart, having read it through so many times in the past half-hour, but still she could not bring herself to a point where she completely understood the smooth and remarkably handsome stranger who was her father. What made it harder, she realised, was the fact that Michael Apollo Scott had more in common with Papa than she cared to admit. Both had deserted their families for a more unfettered existence, but having been deprived of the one's love, and nurtured in the love of the other, she found it hard to see them in the same light. Heracles had understood and forgiven his father; Bethany found it harder.

She intended to show Nikolas the letter, but she had needed a little while to reflect first, for after all the letter was the first informed contact she had had with her own father for more than thirteen years. In fact Nikolas was the first person she saw when she came downstairs, and she handed him the envelope bearing Apollo's black bold handwriting, with a wary little smile. Their last tête-à-tête had ended angrily, only a matter of hours ago, and she had no wish to repeat the experience.

'I've had a letter from my father,' she ventured. 'I'd like you to see it, Nikolas.'

Wordlessly he took it from her and opened out the single sheet, and from the time he took to read it, it was obvious he went through it more than once. Then he folded it and slipped it back into its envelope with almost studied care before he spoke. His first words took her completely by surprise. 'Do you forgive him, Bethany?'

'Why—yes, of course.' She held the letter in both her hands and had to admit herself touched by the tone of it, then raised her eyes to Nikolas's dark and oddly troubled face. 'Don't you think I should forgive him?' she asked. 'It was you who pointed out to me that he was probably more to be pitied than blamed in the present circumstances.'

A brief smile touched his mouth for a moment. 'But that is no guarantee that you'd accept my judgment,' Nikolas told her. 'I'm glad you no longer feel quite so bitter about him, though, Bethany.'

'I don't suppose I shall ever see him again,' she ventured a little wistfully, 'and there doesn't seem much point in hating someone you—well, feel sorry for in a way.'

'No point at all,' Nikolas agreed, and once more she caught a glimpse of a smile. 'You're not very good at sustaining hate, are you, little one?' Her swift questioning look brought another smile, and he shook his head slowly. 'You hated me, I seem to remember, but——' Unexpectedly a hand reached out and rip-

pled strands of tawny hair through his long fingers.
'You don't still hate me, do you, Bethany?'

Her heart was racing, bringing a warmth to her
cheeks that she had no control over, and that wild,
almost wanton sense of need deepened her breathing
until the rise and fall of her breast was as exaggerated
as a deliberate movement. 'You know I don't hate you,'
she whispered.

'Then you forgive me too?' Long brown fingers continued their stroking movement and lightly touched
her neck with their warm tips until she could scarcely
control her trembling. 'For this morning,' he reminded her with a faint smile, 'Theo and I had a very
enlightening talk before he left, and it seems I misjudged you—I'm sorry.'

She shook her head, for it was hard to remember how
bitterly they had blamed one another that morning,
and she more clearly recalled Theo's remarks about
her caring about Nikolas. She did care about him, but
she had not realised quite how much until this moment
as he stood running his fingers through her hair,
lightly, almost deliberately it seemed, arousing a response that must have shown in her eyes before she
concealed them with lowered lids.

Her mouth trembled softly, already anticipating his
kiss; willing and ready to yield because at the moment
she could not think beyond the remembered strength
of his arms and the fierce warmth of his lips. It was
into that wildly wanton mood of anticipation that
Alexia intruded with her gentle, quiet voice.

'Ah, there you are, child; did Theo get away safely?'

To Bethany it seemed like an age since she saw Theo
off on the ferry for Piraeus, and she hastily and reluctantly brought herself back to practicalities. 'Oh
yes, Aunt Alex, although he had to make a dash for it
before Capitan Spiros pulled up the gangway!'

'He'll be home by morning,' said Nikolas, and from
his voice those few intimate moments might never have
happened. It was difficult to see his eyes for the thick
screen of their lashes, but he seemed perfectly normal

and unaffected. 'I have one or two things to do before dinner,' he went on. 'If someone would bring me some coffee to the studio—'

A brief look left little doubt about who he expected to bring him his coffee, and Alexia nodded. 'I'll make some, Niko, and Bethany can bring it to you.'

Catching Bethany's eye for a second, he smiled, his own dark eyes deep and gleaming, so that the burning excitement he brought to life in her tingled through her as she turned to follow Alexia into the kitchen. 'Please do,' he said.

In the kitchen Alexia went about preparing the coffee tray, while Bethany filled the dish of *loukoumi*. 'I didn't know you were back, child,' said Alexia, and Bethany smiled apologetically.

'I'm sorry, Aunt Alex, I should have told you. But I had a letter—from my father, and I wanted to read it while I was alone.'

'Your father?' Bethany nodded. 'Has—— Does Nikolas know?'

'Oh yes.' She made it sound as casual as she could. 'I gave it to him to read. Don't worry, Aunt Alex, we— I shall never see him again.'

'Bethany dear——'

'Oh, it's all right,' Bethany assured her hastily, 'I shan't make a fuss after all this time, although I'm glad I at least spoke to him.' Anxious to change the subject she swiftly passed on to their erstwhile visitor. 'It's going to seem very quiet without Theo, even though he was only here for one day.'

Taking the hint with her customary understanding, Alexia nodded. 'Never mind, child, we shall all be back with the family very soon now.'

Bethany stared at her and her heart was thudding hard and fast suddenly. 'You—you mean—back to Rodos?'

'Yes, of course,' Alexia agreed, and did not attempt to hide her own pleasure at the prospect. 'Takis is due to start at his new school very soon now, and we shall need to settle ourselves before then.'

Quite plainly Alexia had no fault to find with the arrangement, but to Bethany it was a moment she had been dreading ever since they returned from that first visit to Rhodes. And she shied away, as always, from the very idea of leaving Apolidus, presumably for good. 'Are you sure?' she insisted anxiously, although she knew it even before Alexia nodded.

'Yes, of course I'm sure, child,' she told her. 'You must have realised it would come one day, Bethany. You—I wish you wouldn't look so—stricken, child.'

It was something she had put to the back of her mind, determined to banish the very idea, as if by doing so she could prevent it happening. She knew how happy Alexia was about going, but she could think only of her own feelings at the moment. She was half afraid to leave her safe little island, as Nikolas had more than once termed it, but she did not expect anyone else to understand how she felt. Apolidus had always meant something special to her, and for so long now that she felt dismay at the prospect of living anywhere else.

'I don't want to go with you, Aunt Alex!' She appealed to the old lady, but Alexia, it was clear, did not understand her fear; her reluctance to tear herself away from familiar surroundings and be plunged into a whole new way of life. 'I want to stay here in Apolidus, where I know everyone! I have to explain to Niko that he can't——'

'My child, my child, he can't leave you here alone!' Alexia took her hands and held the trembling fingers in her own gentle ones. 'He *won't* leave you here, child, you know he won't.'

'Then I'll just refuse to go—he can't make me! Oh, why can't things just go on being as they were, Aunt Alex? Why?'

Bethany turned swiftly and went hurrying out, just as she had once before, what now seemed like a lifetime ago, and just as she had on that occasion she sought the solitary refuge of the hillside. Just as she had on the evening when her real father had drifted briefly into her life again, she made for the dig that had now been exposed as nothing more than a hollow in the hillside. Instead of sitting down on its rim to brood as she had that evening, however, she made her way down the far side of the hill to the quiet beach where Nikolas had discovered her.

In the evening cool, a light breeze stirred the hair from her neck and threaded its teasing fingers through the silky strands, tossing it into disarray, while the thin cotton dress she wore moulded the contours of her body with caressing firmness. Recalling other firm, gentle hands, she curved her fingers over her breast and tilted her head to defy the taunting familiarity of the breeze.

Theo had tried to warn her, she could see that now, but she had not looked upon the prospect as imminent, choosing to ignore it as she did the question of her marriage, until it became unavoidable. The house was hers, Nikolas had told her that, and if she insisted Nikolas would have to let her stay. Or so she told herself as she walked along the ruffled edge of the tide, but even if she stayed, would she be happy? With Takis and Alexia and Nikolas gone?

'Oh, Niko!'

The cry fell like a sob from her lips and she pressed her hands to her mouth because tears were running down her cheeks and she had never felt as she did now. It wasn't fair of him to snatch her away from everything she loved and put her among strangers. He was heartless, as she had often declared him to be. But if that was so she did not see why she found no pleasure in the thought of Apolidus without him.

The sun in the purpling sky looked exotic and unreal, tinting the sandy-red rocks to a deep crimson with its dying blood and turning the solitary little farmhouse on the hillside to a rich rose pink. Even the darting scallops at the edge of the tide advanced and retreated in ripples of golden-pink before deep purple waves but for the first time Bethany remained unaware and untouched by it all.

She never knew what made her turn her head when she did, but the sight of Nikolas coming along the beach towards her gave her a moment of wild exultation that was beyond anything she could account for. She tossed back her hair, but with her back to the wind it immediately blew forward across her face again and gave her only a striated view of him.

He was walking quite slowly and as she stood there on legs that felt on the point of collapsing under her, Bethany wondered at his leisurely pace, if he came seeking her in anger. Inevitably she attributed his appearance to anger because she had left Alexia to finish preparing the coffee she had promised to take to him, but when he got closer she saw not anger but some indefinable expression she could not understand.

His eyes were shadowed, not just by the approaching night, but by their heavy black lashes, and his mouth looked firm without that angry tightness she had come to dislike so much. He wore no jacket and short sleeves showed bare brown arms swinging easily at his side, the hands loosely rolled.

He stopped just in front of her as Bethany swung round to face him, her eyes downcast. 'What makes you always run away, Bethany?'

There was no anger in his voice either, only a soft note of reproach that was so affecting she hastily caught her bottom lip between her teeth. 'I—I had something on my mind, that's all,' she explained.

'And you preferred to come out here alone rather than come to me and talk it over.' He gave her no time to confirm or deny, but went on with what he had to say as if he had to get it over quickly. 'If you really want to stay on here, Bethany, you can.'

It made no kind of sense, she knew, but Bethany realised that it was not the speech she either expected or wanted to hear, and she gazed at him for a moment in almost shocked silence. Then she shook her head slowly, keeping her eyes on the tell-tale mouth that seemed to have a vulnerable look instead of its customary hardness. 'But if——'

'Aunt Alexia is going and so is Takis, but you know that already. Aunt Alexia has her friends and her family from whom she has isolated herself for the past seven years to care for you and Takis. You cannot expect her to relinquish this chance to go home, nor Takis to give up his schooling.'

Her hands clasped tightly together, Bethany coped with a churning sensation in her stomach as well as a thudding urgency of her heartbeat. 'And you?' she asked, her voice barely above a whisper.

Nikolas met her eyes directly, a deep gleaming darkness showing between narrowed lids. 'I have a business to run, Bethany, and family responsibilities.'

'And you blame me because you've neglected them, and you hate it here! I'm sorry, Nikolas!'

She saw the slightest tightening of his mouth and regretted it more than she had regretted anything in her life before. For all that he managed to speak quietly and seemingly without emotion. 'I brought you back here because it was what you wanted,' he said.

'And you always do what I want!' Her voice quivered, close to tears.

'Yes, damn you!' Nikolas swore, then almost immediately brought his temper under control again. 'Now I have to turn back to reality and think about someone else for a change. Unlike you I can't hide for ever in a rose-coloured cocoon, I have other people to think about! I *have* to go back, Bethany.'

Her anguish showed plainly in huge grey eyes as wide as a child's, and her mouth was tremulous and appealing. But it was an appeal that Nikolas seemed prepared to resist, for he deliberately looked away, gazing at the sun as it slid deeper into the darkening sea.

'And leave me here?' Bethany whispered.

'If it's what you want.'

'It *is*!'

The words were dragged from her and came out as little more than a harsh whisper, but she turned away from him so that he should not see the tears that coursed unchecked down her cheeks. The thought of

facing a future without Nikolas, even if it meant stay-
ing on her precious island, was quite unbearable suddenly, and she wept for the need to choose between
them. When Theo had warned her of just such a situation she had not realised just how fierce and painful
the struggle would be.

Half turning her head, she spoke over her shoulder
in a shiveringly thin voice. 'When—how soon do you
go?'

'In two days.'

It sounded so very final that she bit hard on her
quivering lip. Her eyes shimmered with tears and she
ached for the strength of his arms around her and the
warm excitement of his mouth. When she thought of
all the days, months even years before her, suddenly
the peace and tranquillity that Apolidus had to offer
wasn't enough any more.

She turned quickly, half afraid he might have been
discouraged by her silence, but he still stood in the
same spot, tall and lean and unbelievably dear to her.
'I'm leaving on Saturday, Bethany.' He spoke quietly,
but there was a vibrance in his voice that shattered
her self-control. 'I'll go without you if I have to,
but——'

'No, Niko, no!' Bethany flung herself forward into
his arms, her own arms clasped tightly around him
while she buried her face against the broad warmth of
his chest. And the whispered plea was half lost as she
pressed so close she could feel every muscle that
strained her to him. 'Don't leave me, please don't leave
me!'

One hand stroked long fingers through her hair and
his lips brushed her forehead while he snuggled her
in the deep haven between shoulder and chin. 'If you
won't come with me I must leave you, little one,' Nikolas murmured. 'I have to remember that I have more
family than one small and very beautiful cousin who
will wind me around her little finger if I allow her to.'
His lips kissed lightly, her forehead, cheek and neck,
one hand still stroking her hair. 'I don't want to leave

you, my little one, but if you give me no choice, I must.'

That searing, irresistible longing rose in her again and Bethany rubbed her cheek against the warm body through a thin-textured shirt, her hands reaching up and sliding inside the neck of the shirt. 'Niko.' She looked up at him with her lips parted, soft and eager for his mouth, and Nikolas moaned like a man in torment as he bent his head and took the lure she offered.

Strong gentle hands moulded her softness and he took her mouth with the fierce hunger of a man who has for too long been denied that which he craves—eager, seeking, demanding a response that she gave only too readily, yielding her mouth to a passion that seemed insatiable and sought to draw the very breath from her body. Releasing her lips with lingering slowness, he kissed her throat and the slender softness of her neck, then once again looked down into her face, folding warm flushed cheeks between his palms as he tried to see her in the almost vanished light.

'I shall take you with me,' Nikolas said in a voice that was not only firm but huskily sensual and brought a clamouring urgency to her heartbeat. 'I shall take you if I have to drag you forcibly by your beautiful hair, do you hear me? I shall take no more nonsense from you!'

His strong fingers twined in her hair and he gave it a brief, sharp tug while his smiling mouth breathed warmth on to her lips, and reaching up, Bethany put her arms around his neck. 'I want to come with you,' she whispered huskily, her lips half smiling and shamelessly inviting another kiss. 'I don't want to stay here without you, Niko.'

'I never intended that you should,' he told her with a gleam of white teeth. 'but I wanted you to come to me of your own free will, if you would.'

'And if I hadn't?'

'If you hadn't,' Nikolas told her in a deep quiet voice that both promised and threatened, 'I should have invoked my right as your guardian and followed my cousin's wishes to the letter.'

It was difficult to judge his expression, for the darkness was complete until the moon came up above the thrust of the hilltop. 'Papa?' she asked, leaning back a little on the hands that rested in the small of her back. 'Papa wanted me to marry——'

'Me,' Nikolas agreed, and laughed at her obvious surprise. 'You shouldn't believe all you hear, my precious love. I tried to give Aunt Alex an inkling without telling her outright, just in case you wouldn't have me, but she got the wrong idea and, I gather, passed it on to you.' He sought her mouth in the warm darkness and kissed her long and lingeringly, then pulled her close and rested his face on the softness of her hair. 'That young brother of mine gave me quite a few uneasy moments,' he confessed. 'I thought you might fall in love with him.'

'With Theo?' Bethany considered for a moment, and realised with some surprise that it had never even occurred to her. 'I never thought of falling in love with Theo,' she confided after due consideration. 'I don't know why—he's good-looking and charming, and——'

Nikolas cut short the list of his brother's virtues, using every means at his disposal to persuade her that his claim was the more pressing, and Bethany was in no mind to deny him. 'You'll marry me,' he told her some time later and with a hint of the familiar ruthless insistence.

But Bethany no longer felt the need to defy him seriously. 'Because Papa wanted you to?' she asked, and caught her breath in a shivering little laugh when that ravishing mouth came close again.

'Because *I* want to,' Nikolas insisted, and gripped her tightly. 'And if you're playing your teasing games again——'

'I love you,' Bethany murmured hastily. 'I love you, Niko!' She brushed the hovering mouth with her lips and smiled. 'You're the only one I ever—played those games with, my darling, I promise you, and I just couldn't resist teasing you.'

'And if I didn't love you so much——'

He did not complete the sentence, but buried his mouth in her soft lips again, lips that yielded eagerly as they always did. And for the first time in her life Bethany did not care whether she was in Apolidus or where she was—it didn't matter as long as Nikolas was there too.

# Don't be caught off guard in 1981!

## Be ready—Get prepared Know what's in store

Let
# *Harlequin*
## *Romance Horoscope 1981*
### *be your guide!*

*A delightfully intriguing handbook,*
*specially designed for today's woman,*
*to give you a headstart on 1981.*

# Romance Calendar 1981
*A special guide for those in love!*

# No one
# can hand you success
# on a silver platter...

—— *But* ——

# *Harlequin*
# *Romance Horoscope 1981*

*can help you achieve it for yourself!*

## *Discover...*

★

**how to make the most of your
unique talents**

★

**when to forge ahead to get what
you want**

★

**how to achieve and maintain
satisfying relationships**

★

**exciting glimpses of the future**

*all this and much, much more in*

# *Harlequin*
# *Romance Horoscope 1981*

What sort of man is the best mate for you?
Should you choose a brand-new career?
What are your real inner strengths?
How can you use the precious secret of
timing to achieve success?

*These questions and many others*
*are answered for you in . . .*

# Harlequin
# Romance Horoscope 1981

A lively guide to loving and living
in the year ahead.

Get your own special guide,
the book of your zodiac sign.
Discover what 1981
holds in store for you!

Available now at your favorite store.

# 4
# FREE
# *Harlequin Romances*

# TAKE THESE 4 FREE

## Harlequin Romances

as advertised on TV

Thrill to romantic, aristocratic Istanbul, and the tender love story of a girl who built a barrier around her emotions in ANNE HAMPSON's "Beyond the Sweet Waters" . . . a Caribbean island is the scene setting for love and conflict in ANNE MATHER's "The Arrogant Duke" . . . exciting, sun-drenched California is the locale for romance and deception in VIOLET WINSPEAR's "Cap Flamingo" . . . and an island near the coast of East Africa spells drama and romance for the heroine in NERINA HILLIARD's "Teachers Must Learn."

Harlequin Romances . . . 6 exciting novels published each month! Each month you will get to know interesting, appealing, true-to-life people . . . . You'll be swept to distant lands you've dreamed of visiting . . . . Intrigue, adventure, romance, and the destiny of many lives will thrill you through each Harlequin Romance novel.

## Get all the latest books before they're sold out!

As a Harlequin subscriber you actually receive your personal copies of the latest Romances immediately after they come off the press, so you're sure of getting all 6 each month.

## Cancel your subscription whenever you wish!

You don't have to buy any minimum number of books. Whenever you decide to stop your subscription just let us know and we'll cancel all further shipments.

Your FREE gift includes
- *Anne Hampson* — Beyond the Sweet Waters
- *Anne Mather* — The Arrogant Duke
- *Violet Winspear* — Cap Flamingo
- *Nerina Hilliard* — Teachers Must Learn

# FREE GIFT CERTIFICATE

## and Subscription Reservation

### Mail this coupon today!

**In U.S.A.:**
Harlequin Reader Service
MPO Box 707
Niagara Falls, NY 14302

**In Canada:**
Harlequin Reader Service
649 Ontario Street
Stratford, Ontario
N5A 6W4

### Harlequin Reader Service:

Please send me my 4 Harlequin Romance novels
FREE. Also, reserve a subscription to the 6 NEW
Harlequin Romance novels published each month.
Each month I will receive 6 NEW Romance novels at
the low price of $1.25 each (Total — $7.50 a month).
There are no shipping and handling or any other
hidden charges. I may cancel this arrangement at any
time, but even if I do, these first 4 books are still mine
to keep.

_____

NAME                    (PLEASE PRINT)

_____

ADDRESS

_____

CITY        STATE/PROV.        ZIP/POSTAL CODE

Offer not valid to present subscribers

Offer expires March 31, 1981                    R2356

Prices subject to change without notice.